"It's so like you to cover all your bases," Bedelia said.

Dolph smiled tightly. "That's one way a man gets what he wants."

She stiffened, hesitating, wariness rippling down her spine. "You sound resentful. Won't food turn to acid in your stomach?"

"I'll risk it." The hoarseness in his voice showed his irritation.

Bedelia moved away from him, chin high. "As I recall, you had a tongue like a rapier when you were in a tantrum."

"Why, darling, I'm in a full-blown fury with you." When she turned sharply, he kissed her hard, then released her.

Catching her breath, Bedelia met his gaze. "Didn't you promise me dancing?"

He pulled her into his arms, memory flooding him. Pressing his lips to her hair, he swung her close to his body. "Remember the night we danced on the beach in Nice?"

They'd been naked, for goodness' sake! "Vaguely." Her husky voice gave her away. Heat pulsed through her.

"Then we watched the sunrise on the sea. It was beautiful," Dolph whispered into her hair. Their bodies swayed as one. "Breakfast was—"

"I'm listening to the music," she said quickly.

Dolph had told her he wanted to have her for breakfast. And she'd told him to go ahead and take his fill!

An unseen hand propelled them ever closer. She was whirling with the man and the music into a vortex from which there was no return. . . .

WHAT ARE *LOVESWEPT* ROMANCES?

They are stories of true romance and touching emotion. We believe those two very important ingredients are constants in our highly sensual and very believable stories in the *LOVESWEPT* line. Our goal is to give you, the reader, stories of consistently high quality that may sometimes make you laugh, sometimes make you cry, but are always fresh and creative and contain many delightful surprises within their pages.

Most romance fans read an enormous number of books. Those they truly love, they keep. Others may be traded with friends and soon forgotten. We hope that each *LOVESWEPT* romance will be a treasure—a "keeper." We will always try to publish

LOVE STORIES YOU'LL NEVER FORGET
BY AUTHORS YOU'LL ALWAYS REMEMBER

The Editors

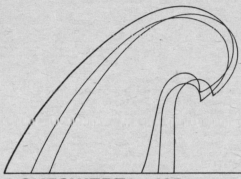

LOVESWEPT® • 425

Helen Mittermeyer
Men of Ice:
Frozen Idol

BANTAM BOOKS
NEW YORK • TORONTO • LONDON • SYDNEY • AUCKLAND

FROZEN IDOL

A Bantam Book / September 1990

*LOVESWEPT® and the wave device are registered
trademarks of Bantam Books, a division of
Bantam Doubleday Dell Publishing Group, Inc.
Registered in U.S. Patent
and Trademark Office and elsewhere.*

*If you would be interested in receiving protective vinyl
covers for your Loveswept books, please write to this
address for information:*

> *Loveswept
> Bantam Books
> P. O. Box 985
> Hicksville, NY 11802*

ISBN 0-553-44056-X

Published simultaneously in the United States and Canada

---

*Bantam Books are published by Bantam Books, a division
of Bantam Doubleday Dell Publishing Group, Inc. Its trademark, consisting of the words "Bantam Books" and the
portrayal of a rooster, is Registered in U.S. Patent and
Trademark Office and in other countries. Marca Regis-
trada. Bantam Books, 666 Fifth Avenue, New York, New
York 10103*

PRINTED IN THE UNITED STATES OF AMERICA

OPM   0 9 8 7 6 5 4 3 2 1

One

The café was off the beaten track in Nice, and frequented by the locals, not tourists. That had been the attraction for Dolph Wakefield.

It had been a helluva day. Nearly everything had gone wrong, back-to-back. Drinking wine and arm wrestling with some fishermen helped relieve some of the sourness of the day. No one in the café knew or cared that he was an actor in the movie that was being filmed in the area.

Long after closing he and his newfound cronies left the café, raucous and reeling, the threats of the innkeeper following them. As his fellow drinkers went off, Dolph assumed, to their homes, he staggered to his car alone.

Fuzzy-headed, he climbed into the vintage Jaguar he'd been able to lease rather cheaply. It swallowed gasoline like a thirsty camel, but it had pickup and climbing power.

Dolph sped away from the city, enjoying the muted roar under the hood. He had to drive up into the hills; the villa where he was staying clung to the hillside like one of the native goats. The challenge of navigating the curving road without lessening speed was a potent delight, though he would have been the first to admit that much of his heady feeling came from drinking pungent peasant wine.

Life was sweet at that moment. He'd almost forgotten the frustrations of the day. Totting up the good things was far more pleasurable. He was becoming better known. His work was being noticed; he was offered more choice parts. And someone else was paying for him to spend time in Europe. He'd always loved the Continent. He'd gone to school in France and Germany when his father had been an ambassador, spoke several languages, and was thoroughly at home in most European countries. What could be better?

Pressing the accelerator to the floor, he sped around a steep curve.

When he heard a grunt, he thought it was his imagination. The second time he heard it, he pulled over as close to the cliffside as he could, stopping the car, and looked into the crawl space behind him. "What the hell?" He blinked, trying to wipe out the vision of the woodsprite in his car.

"No need to get all puffed, up," the sprite said. "I'm the one getting thrown around like a rag doll because of your stupid driving."

"Stupid driving?" Dolph stared at the girl with the cropped auburn hair, pointed chin, and sparkling eyes. "I'll have you know I've driven in the Mille Miglia." Why the hell was he explaining to her? A throbbing started behind his eyes. "Just what are you doing in my car?"

"Hiding. My concierge's son was after me. He said he wanted to collect the money I owe his mother. I think he wanted more than that."

"Don't you have a job?" How old was she? No more than eighteen. And she was American.

"I'm looking for a job," she said. "I'm trying to get on that movie set they have here. Do you know the one I mean?"

"I think so." Dolph got out of the car, closing his eyes against his headache. The red wine he'd been downing was locally pressed, new and lethal. "Would you like to ride up front? Where am I supposed to be taking you?" Hell, why should he ask her? He should be flaming mad at the imposition. He noticed when she climbed into the front that she had long legs, their slender curves enhanced by the shabby cotton shorts she wore. He cursed silently. She was a child.

"Anywhere is fine," she said, "as long as Pierre doesn't find me. You needn't look like that. I fully intend to pay my concierge as soon as I get the money. I just don't want to wrestle with her son."

"How did you get to Europe if you have no money?" Not that he cared. His headache was building. He restarted the car and accelerated up the mountain road.

"My father left me a small amount of money in

his will. Hey, take it easy. I don't have a death wish."

"I might have one after taking you on as a passenger."

"Hangover?"

"What's your name?"

"Bedelia Fronsby."

"Good Lord, couldn't you make up a more original name than that? It sounds like something out of a gothic novel."

"Really?" Bedelia said stiffly. "Sorry about that. But it happens to be my real name."

"Did your parents hate you?"

"Stop sniping. *You're* the one who's badly strung-out and reeking of wine. And you'll be getting an elephant of a headache that will last all day tomorrow." Bedelia chortled. "Serves you right for making fun of my name."

"Your name doesn't need help from me. It's ridiculous as it is."

"My, you are touchy," Bedelia muttered, gazing out the passenger window. It had been ridiculous to get in his car, she thought, but it had seemed like the logical hiding place at the time. Pierre would have never looked for her in a Jaguar, even an old one.

"I had money," she said after a moment, "when my college roommate and I got here two months ago. But she flew home when she got sick, and then I lost my backpack. You see, we had biked through France, intending to continue on to Italy . . . "

He yawned, and she closed her mouth.

Silence fell between them.

A couple of miles later Dolph swung between two stone pillars onto a hilly hairpin-curve drive. He didn't slow down, but sped through the many twists on the narrow road. At the top he skidded into another turn before swishing to a halt in a spray of pebbles.

"Here we are," he said. "If you can close your mouth long enough not to interrupt me, you can use the couch in my lounge. Otherwise you're on your own."

"My, aren't we generous."

"Now, look—"

"Okay, okay." Bedelia stared at the white villa outlined in the moonlight. It was certainly better accommodations than she'd had for the last two months. And it had been scary more than once being on her own. At least this stranger was an American. Of course, he could be an axe murderer on the run.

"It's a pretty barn of a place," she said as they got out of the car. "Do you like fish in the morning? I could go down to the sea and get us something. The boats come in early." He was good-looking, she mused. At least she wouldn't have to wrestle him. He was clearly a washout. Bedelia chuckled.

"Please don't." Dolph shuddered, one hand rubbing his forehead. "I have a day off tomorrow. I'm sleeping in until the sun goes down. If you stay, move quietly."

She nodded. "You know, you smell like a winery before they clean the vats."

"And you would know how that smells?"

"Sure. I worked in one. Want me to tell you how

it smelled after the skins were in the sun for a day?"

"Quiet, brat, and good night."

"Can I have some sheets?" She followed him into the villa that smelled of bay leaves and sweet basil. Nice.

"Huh? What? Oh. Try the linen closet down the hall." He gestured and turned away.

"You'll have to show me," she said doggedly.

"I'll throw you into the sea instead," he muttered, but walked down the hall. Jungle drums beat a ragged cadence from the front of his skull to the back.

"Maybe you shouldn't drink at all. You might be allergic. You certainly look awful."

"I drive awful, I look awful. Is there anything else you'd like to critique?" He threw open the cupboard and pointed to the stacks of linen.

"I'm only trying to give you some good advice," she said loftily. "You should probably see a psychiatrist about that personality disorder."

"Now my mind is gone. Great. Good night. And don't say anything else."

"All right, if that's the way you feel."

"Dammit, Bedelia, shut up."

"Grouch," she said to his back as he climbed the stairs.

Dolph didn't pay attention. He staggered into his room, stripped off his clothes, and fell face forward on the bed.

The next morning Dolph was disturbed by sun flashing in his eyes and the unholy sound of his Jaguar motor screaming. "Ohh," he groaned as he levered himself out of bed, pushing aside the mosquito netting that Lorette, the housekeeper, insisted on draping over each bed. "Dammit to hell!" he shouted, "Who's making all the noise? It's . . ." He squinted at his watch. "It's eight o'clock in the morning."

Staggering to the window, which was wide open, the drawn net drapes blowing in on streams of sunlight, he leaned over the balcony. "What in hell is going on?"

Down on the drive, Bedelia was standing beside the open hood of his car. She looked up at him. "Don't you do anything but swear? Really." Turning back to the car, she peered at the motor. "I've cleaned and replaced your plugs. Now I'm testing the carburetor. Don't you know how to handle these high-compression jobs? Drove the Mille Miglia! My Aunt Fanny," she pronounced scathingly.

Cursing and holding his head, Dolph tried to go back to sleep, but he couldn't for the noise.

Finally, after taking a thirty-minute shower, he decided he would go for a swim. Then he would strangle the waif with the dippy Victorian name. That might ease the throbbing in his head.

Downstairs, he met the housekeeper in the front hall.

"M. Duff," she said in her French-accented English, "I am sorry about the noise." Lorette shrugged, rolling her eyes. "I tried to tell 'er, but the *jeune fille* said you would not mind."

"I do mind, but it's not your fault. I'm going down to the sea. I'll take the Rover."

"*Ah, oui.* The sea is nice today. *Peut-être* you will want the sailboard? It is in the boathouse, *m'sieur.*"

"Thanks, Lorette. Don't bother telling the brat where I've gone." He loped down the hall to the rear courtyard and the garages.

"Hi," Bedelia said as soon as he stepped outside. "Where you going? Swimming? I'll come with you. I've finished with the Jag."

Dolph stared at her. "You have grease on your nose, cheeks, legs, and arms, and probably on the back of your shorts."

She glared at him. "And who do you think did the car? The tooth fairy? Of course I have grease on me, ninny. A swim will wash me off."

"You don't have your suit."

She shrugged. "I usually swim in the nude. But if you're going to one of the suited beaches, I'll swim in my shorts."

Visions of her tall slender body against the sparkling sea had him reeling. "You'll get grease on the upholstery of the Rover," he said distractedly. "It isn't mine."

"I'll sit on a clean rag." She sprinted into the garage, then reappeared in an instant waving a large square of cloth. "Let's go."

Nonplussed not only by Bedelia herself but by how she was able to flummox him, Dolph stood immobile, staring.

"Want me to drive?" she asked.

That snapped him out of his daze. "No!" he said abruptly, climbing into the trucklike vehicle.

She scrambled in, and he backed out with a squeal of tires. The jouncing punished his head.

"You don't drive this any better than you did the Jag," she told him succinctly.

"Bedelia!" His head was twice its normal size, the jungle drums at full throttle.

"All right, simmer down. My, you are hyper. Did you take aspirin for your hangover? That could help."

"I don't want to discuss it." He shot down the drive to the main road, then took a short cut to the marina.

"Wow! This is wild," Bedelia exclaimed as they flew down the road that was little more than a cart track. "Go for it!"

Dolph glanced at his passenger, not able to stem a chuckle at her glee. "You're the damnedest daredevil I've ever seen."

"How can you say that? You hardly know me. I've never done anything out of the norm with you." Piqued, she lifted her chin and stared out the windshield.

"No? What do you call getting in a car with a stranger at three in the morning?" The rush of air was alleviating some of his discomfort, though his mouth felt like the bottom of a birdcage.

"A stranger who was inebriated, at that," she added. "You're right. I'd call it a combination of desperation and lunacy." He was pretty clear-headed to remember anything of last night, she thought. And he hadn't come on to her either. Unusual man.

"Thank you for that," Dolph said sardonically, parking the Rover near the boathouse. He looked at the sea with satisfaction. It was rolling and fresh, white-tipped waves rushing to the beach. It would be fast going on the sailboard. "Be careful swimming. There's an undertow at times. I'm going to take out a sailboard."

"I'll take one out too."

"Can you handle it? These are full-size." He got out of the car and looked at her over the roof.

"Can you?"

Annoyed, he stared back at her for a long moment, then turned and strode to the boathouse. He took two boards down from the wall and handed one to her. "Good luck."

"Thanks." She blocked his way when he would have left the boathouse. "You never told me your name or what you do. And I think it's about time you did. I know this is your day off. Are you a bartender, or a waiter in one of the hotels?"

"I act. My name is Dolph Wakefield."

She frowned. "No kidding. An actor, huh?" Finally she nodded slowly. "I have heard of you, but you're no top banana."

Glaring at her, he shoved the board under his arm and stalked from the boathouse. "And you're a tart-tongued brat."

"I heard that."

He sprinted across the hot sand into the sea, gasping at its coldness. In moments he was paddling out to catch the strong gusts and swirls of sea wind. Though the days were hot and getting hotter, there was generally a breeze on the water. Today there were winds. He found good ones out some distance.

Standing on the board and bringing up the sail, he looked behind him. Bedelia had finished greasing herself with something and had taken up her board. His own bucked under him, and he turned away, catching the gust. Soon he was zooming along the shoreline.

Laughing out loud, he strained to pull the sail into an even better position. His speed increased.

As he arced around to cut across the waves, he gasped at the sudden sight of Bedelia. He hadn't reckoned on her making it out so fast, certain the long board and tall sail would be too much for her to handle. She'd come up on his blind side, and he was headed right for her.

Throwing himself backward, he corrected the angle, but a small wave took the bow and lifted it to the sky. He slid, fought to stay erect, and failed. The loose board sliced through the air as he went down, his arms and legs flailing.

Surfacing, he spat water and swiped at his salt-wet eyes. He scanned the area for his board.

"I have it," Bedelia called. "Boy, you do a very Hollywoodish pratfall, Wakefield." She laughed at him, lying down on her board and holding on to the line of his.

"Thank you," he said stiffly. He had an urge to kill her . . . and kiss her. He shook away the uncomfortable thoughts. Bedelia was a child, for Pete's sake.

"Lighten up, big man," she said. "Most people look like a jackass now and then. It probably won't be the last time for you—"

Dolph saw her eyes widen as she understood the look in his.

"Now wait a minute. Can't you take a joke? Hey! Stay away from me. Wakefield!" As he started toward her, panic rose unbidden in her. She remembered another time, when her stepbrother had tackled her in the water. The thought gave impetus to her movements.

Dolph dove under her board as Bedelia scrambled to her feet. She yanked on the sail, intent on making a getaway. Thrusting upward, he broke the surface and grabbed her leg, unbalancing her. Then he tugged hard and pulled her down into the water with him.

She fought him, struggling to free herself. Then panic swamped her, and she flailed wildly. He was holding her under. She was drowning!

Dolph's grim delight at having the upper hand for once with the waif of the night faded when he saw real fear, not laughter, in her eyes. She was taking water, not holding her breath and relaxing.

Shooting to the surface, he cradled her, letting her catch her breath. "Bedelia, look at me. I'm sorry. I had no intention of hurting or frightening you. I was just teasing. Look at me. Please." He supported the two of them, treading water easily, the two boards bobbing away unnoticed. He held her close but loosely, feeling a sharp pain at her anguish. "Please look at me."

Sobs shaking her, she shook her head. "Let me go. I have to go."

"No, I can't let you go, honey. You're shaking." As one of the boards went by, he grabbed for it. "Here. Get on." He gently lifted her on, then swam away to retrieve the other board.

Before he could return to her, he saw her stand, take up the sail, and head for shore. Shocked at the fear he'd seen in her eyes and angry at himself, he clambered on his board and almost bent the sail double in an effort to catch her.

They reached the shore almost at the same time, running up on the beach.

As though she realized he was right at her heels, Bedelia turned to face him, her hands curled into fists. No one was going to intimidate her.

"Bedelia," he said softly, remorse filling him. He'd wiped away all that beautiful spirit, her liveliness and inner fire, in one stupid, injudicious move. Why had it affected her so? "Talk to me."

"I'm leaving," she said woodenly. "Stay away."

"No. And I won't let you leave." He saw how she cringed when he approached, glancing over her shoulder as though looking for an escape route. He stopped inches away from her. "I didn't mean to hurt you. I wouldn't do that. Please don't go away like this. There's no need to fear me."

She gazed at him, shaking her head as tears fell onto her cheeks.

Dolph had never felt such pity, such regret. Cautiously he reached out to her. When she didn't move away, he enfolded her loosely in his arms, crooning to her. "Shh, it's all right. Nothing's going to hurt you."

Sobs shook Bedelia. No matter how hard she tried to stifle them, they rolled out of her. Surprised and helpless, she sagged against Dolph. Her mind told her to run, but not one atom of her being obeyed her.

He held her tighter, resting his chin on her hair. "Shh, honey, don't. I was irked, but it was only a joke. I swear I didn't mean to hurt you. I'm so sorry. It was stupid. Why were you so scared? Can you tell me that?"

Shaking her head, Bedelia didn't look up. She didn't want to discuss her stepbrother Orton . . . or her family . . . or how alone she'd been.

"Bedelia, if I promise not to pry, will you stay with me?" It was paramount to keep her with him, to comfort her, not to let her run away and be alone again.

She shook her head once more.

"Please, Bedelia. I want a chance to square myself with you, be your friend." He lifted her chin and stroked her tear-streaked face. "We'd better shower or we'll have more than salt bloom on us. Seawater stings the eyes after a time." He rubbed her back, speaking to her softly. The words didn't matter. She had stopped pushing against him, trying to free herself.

For several minutes neither moved or spoke. The silence was broken only by the raucous cries of the gulls . . . and Bedelia's long shuddering sighs.

At last she spoke. "When I was younger, I used to tease my stepbrother," she blurted on trembling breaths. "Each time, he would retaliate a little more. Then, when I was twelve and we were vacationing at a lake, he held me under the water. I fought him, and he broke my arm. He was able to convince my stepmother and father that it had been an accident. I avoided him as much as I could after that, and didn't tease him anymore."

Dolph touched her face with one finger. "A wise decision." At that moment he could have killed her stepbrother without a qualm.

She let him lead her to one of the beach showers and stood, head lolling, while he sluiced her down thoroughly. Then he hitched her over a bit and did the same to himself. He didn't release her.

After returning the sailboards to the boathouse, he took her hands and looked at her. "Would you like to go for a drive?"

"No," she said dully. "I think I'd better leave."

His heart plummeted to his feet. Shocked at the bereft feeling she'd spawned by her words, he just stared at her. "Please. Forgive me."

"All right." Bedelia turned away. It was time, she told herself, that she make some plans to go back to the United States. She could call her lawyer, Brooks, for a loan. But then Orton might find her. . . .

"Don't leave me," Dolph said, his voice taut with anguish. He hadn't known her twenty-four hours, but the pain he experienced at the thought of her leaving was real.

Blinking in surprise, Bedelia looked at him. "I'm not leaving to punish you. It's just better this way. I should check with the airlines about going back to the United States. . . ." Her voice trailed off, and she shook her head.

"Let me get a picnic from the village," he said quickly. When she started to say no, he hurried on. "We'll only talk if you choose. We'll look at the sea and the birds flying overhead. We'll watch the yachts go in and out of the harbor, and we'll drink the local grape juice, ice-cold. And we'll have olives and a loaf of bread as long as your arm." She opened her mouth to speak again, but he pressed one finger lightly to her lips. "The man in the sausage store makes his own sausage, and we can eat it with goat cheese." When he saw a dimple flash, a tentative smile appear, happiness washed over him. "Please."

He'd never begged anyone before. But he needed Bedelia with him for numerous, nebulous reasons. None of which he cared to examine at that moment. At her slight nod, he sagged with relief. "Ah, listen, you'd better take off your wet things." Now that he knew she was going to stay, he had to force himself not to stare at her breasts, easily visible beneath her soaked cotton camisole. "Maybe you could wear a shirt of mine that's in the Rover until we can dry these in the sun."

"No underwear," Bedelia said reasonably. It was amazing how he'd reassured her, she mused. The fear was fading fast.

Stymied, Dolph stared at her. "Ah, right. But . . . my shirt is a heavy cotton, and it will probably come to your knees. Perfectly respectable. It should be all right," he said tentatively. "I'm just going to wear a T-shirt and cutoffs. We'll dry everything as fast as we can. Then if you get uncomfortable, you can change."

She smiled up at him. "All right."

His heart turned over at her smile. Inhaling shakily, he reached out to her. She stepped back, and his arms dropped to his sides.

As she walked to the Rover, he followed right behind her, still uncertain which way she'd jump. It was like walking on hot coals. And he wasn't even sure why she was so important.

He got his shirt for her, then watched as she

returned to the boathouse, her tall, lean body swaying, naturally provocative. Never had he felt so unsure of himself, so thrown off course. Bedelia was a witch, a svelte, curvaceous child who intrigued him as no one ever had.

Common sense dictated that he encourage her to leave him, as she'd said she wanted to. But a corner had been turned in those moments in the water. Until he could sort out his own feelings, assuage his guilt and delve into her fears, he wasn't going to be parted from her.

Dolph scampered into his own clothes and was standing next to the Rover when she came out of the boathouse. He kept his gaze on her face, not on his plaid shirt, which teasingly covered her body. Her innocent sensuality sent him reeling.

The drive into the nearest old town, one of the many that seemed to run into each other along the narrow, winding roads in southern France, took only minutes.

As soon as they found a spot, they parked. They bought bread at the pâtisserie, then walked to the shop where the man made the sausage just behind the counter. When Bedelia laughed at a boy delivering bread from his bike, his basket piled so high with the deliciously aromatic loaves that he couldn't see over it, Dolph felt a sweet happiness.

He purchased a wicker basket in the shop with stainless-steel flatware and cloth napkins. They filled it with the bread and sausage. The shopkeeper ladled dripping olives into a jar from a huge barrel, then secured fruit juice and mineral water in a net bag.

With their purchases in hand, Dolph and Bedelia strolled back to the car. As he opened her door for her, she smiled at him. His heart turned over and squeezed tight in his chest. He was delighted to see her gradually ascend from her blue mood.

"Are you hungry?" he asked as he settled behind the wheel.

She sank back against the upholstery and sighed. "And thirsty." And happy! she thought in amazement.

It had never mattered so much to Dolph if someone else was sharing his enjoyment. Now it was all-important. He wanted to look at Bedelia all the time. He ignored the clamor in his brain that told him involving himself with her was foolish, that he couldn't. She was so young. Besides, at the moment his world was work as he strove to reach a pinnacle in his profession. It was all-important. Wasn't it?

Dolph cruised slowly out of the town and up into the hills. By the time he'd reached a plateau high above the sea, Bedelia was dozing.

Dolph knew instinctively that the black fear instigated by her stepbrother was a recurring nightmare. It had not been expunged but only tamped down for a time. He wanted to know all about her, find a way to blot out the dark side.

Worry pierced the bubble of his happiness. Did she get enough sleep? Was she well? She was fine! he told himself. He'd seen her with the board. She was in good condition. He had to smile when he recalled how well she'd handled the sailboard. It was a strange sensation to be overflowing with goodwill, with affection, with caring. For the last few years ambition, determination, and purpose had been the prime forces in his life.

Bedelia was a new experience. He had some good friends he saw socially, and he'd been content with that. Basically a loner, happy with his own company, he'd never sought an entanglement of any kind. Temporary liaisons with women satisfied him. His only family were cousins who lived in England, and he didn't see them often. An only child, he'd been raised with all the advantages. Many of his younger years had been spent in private schools. He'd lost his parents when he was twenty, and he'd grieved. But because of his father's travels for the government, he hadn't spent much time with them.

Bedelia was sunshine and warmth, and he'd never even known those things were missing from his life.

Up in the hills a strong wind blew. They spread out a blanket in the shelter of a rock and set out the contents of the wicker basket and net bag.

Munching on fresh island olives that had been steeped in oil and vinegar and were redolent of herbs and garlic, they sat back against the rock and scanned the sky and sea.

"I like the sound of silence," Bedelia whispered.

Dolph smiled, then leaned over impulsively and kissed her cheek. He held his breath until she smiled back at him. "Describe the sound of silence."

"Oh, you know. The pulsations of the air, the whisper of a breeze through leaves, the call of a bird, dry grass crackling underfoot, breathing, sometimes even the soft hiss of rain on a hot rock."

"Yes." He could see and feel it all. She'd made the world come alive for him in that instant, as though for all of his twenty-nine years he'd ignored much of the planet. Not only hadn't he paused to smell the roses, he'd ignored their existence altogether. With Bedelia he began to put it into shape, to taste, absorb. . . . And she'd wrought this in him in less than a day.

They slid lower down the rock, sipping fruit juice laced with mineral water, their shoulders touching, conversation desultory.

Dolph imitated a bird. Bedelia made the sound of dry grass. They both laughed.

"I'm better," he said.

"Just because you're an actor doesn't make you better," she argued.

When they fell asleep, it was as though on signal.

Opening his eyes, Dolph knew where he was at once. Staring at the sky, he was at peace knowing he was with Bedelia. He took a blade of grass and brushed it across her nose until she woke.

"That one cloud is a lamb," she murmured.

It had been a long time, she thought, since she'd felt lazy, relaxed, warm. She'd been on a never-ending treadmill, it seemed, since her parents had contracted a rare fatal disease while on safari in Africa. She'd been in her freshman year at college, and at first she'd felt safe there. Then Orton had begun driving her crazy with his pestering. She should marry him, he told her. She should turn over her annuity to him. She shouldn't spend so much money. . . . On and on he went, never letting up. She'd disliked him when their parents were alive, and after their death, he'd become even more obnoxious. She'd been on a frantic escape route ever since. Orton was maddening, like water dripping on stone. If she stayed around him too long, she'd be worn away. Now she didn't trust anyone completely or want to involve herself with anyone. But with Dolph . . . she felt so unwound, so loose.

"And that's a ewe," she said.

"A me?" smiling, Dolph followed the direction of her finger, liking the sensation of waking up next to her.

"Ewe like a sheep, silly." Her laughter echoed in the small cozy corner of the rock that cocooned them.

"That one's a donkey," he said. It was wonderful to lie back and scan the blue sky and fluffy snow-white clouds. Having Bedelia at his side made him feel like a boy . . . but there were other feelings that were not at all childlike. He struggled to shut down that part of his thinking.

"Wakefield, you must be blind. That's a train." Bedelia chuckled, feeling as carefree as she had when she'd been small, before Orton had come into her life. Dolph Wakefield had given her back the happiness of childhood, and she savored it.

"Not that one, *that* one," he said, pointing with his foot.

He became as absorbed in the game as Bedelia, arguing hotly when she didn't agree with his assessment of the shape of a particular cloud. Competitively he fought to find the best shape.

"You act as though you'd never played 'name the cloud' before," she said, rolling over on her stomach, a slight frown on her face. "Were you a deprived child?"

Maybe he had been. He lay on his stomach too, so that they were facing each other. "Actually there was always enough money and toys. And my parents were loving." Yes, he'd had life's luxuries aplenty but not a lot of its exquisite simplicities, like time, play, conversation, sharing. "We traveled, and I liked that. My parents had a lifelong interest in people, so I was exposed to a variety of languages and cultures."

His mother and father had loved him in their casual, absent way, but their commitment to their respective countries had been paramount. His father had been an ambassador to the Court of St. James's, as well as other countries. His mother had been descended from a powerful titled English family. *Duty* had been a big word in their lives. Dolph had been alone a great deal, but he'd never been lonely. It was a blow to realize he'd be lonely without Bedelia. And he'd just met her!

"Have your parents seen you act?" she asked.

"My parents have been dead for several years, but yes, they did see me act once or twice." Though they'd struggled to mask it, he'd known they were disappointed in his choice of career. They'd been movers and shakers who expected him to be cut from the same cloth. Still, they'd supported his decision.

Dolph had known many people. Most he liked. Some he didn't like. A few he despised. But none of them had slipped under his guard. No one had ever gotten as close to his inner self as Bedelia. He didn't question why that didn't put him off, why he didn't turn his back on her, why he didn't put up a shield.

He looked up at the sky again, pointing to another cloud. "That's you."

"Nah."

"It is." He turned his head and stared at her again. "Are you a witch, Bedelia Fronsby?"

"I've been called worse."

Dolph wasn't even sure when he'd taken her hand. He brought it to his mouth and kissed each of her knuckles. She smiled at him, and his heart turned over in his chest, his insides contracting with a piercing joy.

Two

Bedelia had been with Dolph for two weeks, and they hadn't exchanged a great deal of personal information. Once that wouldn't have been pertinent. Now Dolph was irked. He was eager for any detail, any scrap of information that would tell him more about the person who'd taken over his thoughts.

He'd never lived in such close proximity to a woman unless they were lovers. His intimacy with Bedelia consisted of an occasional kiss on the cheek or hand. Nothing more. Yet he'd never felt so entwined with anyone, so committed. Far from being disturbed by that, he relished it.

Though Dolph knew little about Bedelia, she was like a part of him. She'd seeped through his pores in a mysterious, magical osmosis.

Common sense told him to shuck her. His personal life had always been walled against the outside. At least he should consider having her investigated. She could be a tabloid reporter, or a groupie who could bring down the fragile pyramid his career was forming. No! Dolph buried all the voices that told him to be cautious. He was happy. Bedelia had unchained him, given him laughter and serenity.

That she'd managed to filter through the overriding ambition he had for his craft amazed him. Where once he would gladly have worked hours getting scene right, he now was impatient with anyone or anything that caused delays. He wanted to get a scene done in one take, be letter-perfect in his lines. Finishing on time got him home to see Bedelia.

Dolph had always tried to be ready for a scene. Now he was exacting in every nuance, so that his performance was on-target every time. During breaks and lunch he studied and perfected his moves. When the shoot went well, he could hurry home while it was still light. He and Bedelia often sailed in the evening and watched the sun go down on the sea.

As he drove home in the early evening, he always worried she might have gone, as she had said she would. Relief was immense when he saw her.

He couldn't bring himself to question his motives or feelings. Acknowledging that Bedelia was at least ten years younger than he didn't sway his determination to keep her close to him. Emotions could be sorted out later. Now he wanted to be with her, and he sensed she felt the same. No words of commitment had been exchanged. None were needed.

Stones sprayed up around the car when he skidded to a stop in front of the villa.

He rushed into the house, stopping short when he saw Lorette. "Where is she?"

Lorette's Gallic shrug was accompanied by a rolling of the eyes. "Where else would she be? The garden, of course. She is turning it into a vegetable heaven."

"*You* like vegetables. So do I."

Lorette shrugged again. "I do. And getting them from my own garden will save money." Her eyes gleamed with a martial light. "That thief at the market will no longer be stealing from us."

"Good." Dolph didn't stay to hear the diatribe aimed at the greengrocer in the town. He sprinted down the hall to the kitchen, then out through the back door to the walled garden. "Hey," he called when he saw her. "You're getting burned."

Bedelia turned and smiled, swiping at her red face with the sleeve of her cotton smock. "Hi."

"Come out of the sun. You'll get heatstroke."

"I'm almost done. How was your day?" She moved into the shade of dusty grapevines.

Dolph noticed how those vines were no longer choked by weeds, that the melon plants, off by themselves, were curling around wooden stakes. Varied plants now grew straight and unencumbered. Obviously the garden had been started years before, and just as obviously it had been neglected. But Bedelia had cleared away the thick undergrowth, and the perennial plants and herbs were lush and tall. "I don't want you working so hard," he said sternly.

"I thought you were going to tell me about your day." Her teeth flashed in her dirt-smudged face.

Dolph had an urge to kiss her and forced himself to step back. "My day. Let's see, we did some exciting things. Shot one scene ten times, struggled with another one that never did work out." When she laughed, he was delighted. Telling her about his work was such an intimate thing since he rarely shared it with anyone. It wasn't just because she seemed interested, but he wanted her to know about his dreams and goals. That was another new feeling. "Now tell me what you did, Farmer Brown." When she stuck her tongue out at him, his heart pounded, though he laughed back at her.

She waved her arm. "Look for yourself. Tomorrow I'm going to put compost in the back section and plant some late tomatoes and onions." It warmed her all over to have him beside her after the day was done. When he left her in the morning, sometimes she felt downright teary.

Dolph shook his head. "Is that what you do in the States? Farm?" Her startled glance made him regret the question. "Hey, let's take a swim, then go out in the boat."

"I'm awfully dirty."

She looked down at herself, as though studying her clothes, but Dolph knew she was hiding her expression from him.

"We'll both wash in the sea," he said. "I'll give you five minutes." He turned away, hoping she wouldn't balk.

Suddenly she streaked past him. "Last one to

the car gets to carry the picnic basket, set it out, and clean up."

Mouth agape, Dolph watched her for a second. Then, yelping with frustration, he was after her.

Arms akimbo, Lorette watched them clatter through her kitchen. "You are children, both of you."

"Get the basket ready, Lorette," Dolph called to her. "I'll pick it up in the front hall."

"*Ah, oui, the games you play.*"

In minutes the two of them were out of their rooms. Bedelia was slightly ahead as they rushed for the stairs.

Dolph flipped onto the ornate banister and slid down past her to the front hall.

"Cheater!" she yelled in frustration.

He reached the car mere seconds before her, slipping under the wheel and grinning at her.

Leaning on the window of the driver's side, Bedelia looked down at him, their faces inches apart. "For two pins I'd bite your nose."

"Feel free," he said huskily.

When she leaned closer, he tilted his head and her mouth met his.

"Cheater," she muttered.

The kiss was brief, a mere grazing of lips, no more.

Electric shocks jolted through Dolph. Hot knives pierced his armor, his skin, his inner life.

Bedelia felt as if her every muscle turned to water. She pulled back, swallowing hard, her gaze sliding away. "Well . . . well, that was almost like a bite, right?' she stuttered. "Let's go." Ducking her head, she hurried around the front of the car and got into the passenger seat.

"Got everything?" Dolph asked. His ears were ringing; his flesh stung and itched. He burned and froze.

"I think so."

He sped down the drive, a mix of fear, elation, shock, and bewilderment making his handling of the car erratic.

Bedelia stared at the windshield as though she couldn't take her gaze from it. Chaos whirled within her, her heart and brain sending mixed messages. She loved him. She hated him. Was there anything in between?

When Dolph parked at the marina, she was out of the car in a flash. He raced after her. "Bedelia!"

"Gone swimming," she caroled over her shoulder. She dropped her bag and peeled off her shirt and cutoffs almost without pausing.

Sprinting across the hot sand, she threw herself into the sea, Dolph right at her heels.

They swam side by side out into the cool depths.

She flipped over on her back, spewing water out of her mouth, then sighing. "That's wonderful. Some of that soil was imbedded in my pores, I'm sure of it."

He swam closer to her. "Then stop working so hard, and hire someone to do the bull work for you."

"Hire someone? That's an awful waste of money. Besides, what if they're incompetent? I'd end up doing the work anyway."

He touched her arm. "Did I make you uncomfortable when I kissed you?"

"If that was a kiss, Wakefield, I'd say you're all washed up as a heartthrob." She turned over again and dived, thrusting her body down into the wine-colored depths.

Dolph dived with her. When she popped to the surface, he was right there. "Damn you, hold still. I didn't want to upset you."

"You didn't. I liked it, what little there was." She grinned. "But I can do better."

"So can I."

"Let's."

"You're a child," he said hoarsely.

"I'm not, you know. A couple of my friends in college were married this year and . . ." Her voice trailed off as she remembered her friends' May wedding. She'd hated it when Orton had showed up at the reception. His insistence that she return home with him had sent her hot footing it for Europe.

"Tell me," Dolph said.

"It's nothing. I dropped out this year."

"Go back in the fall, redo what you have to, and push on with your studies."

Her smile was twisted. "Oh? It's easy for you to say. You've finished with all that stuff."

"Some of the best times of my life were spent in college."

"We were talking about kissing."

"Were we?"

"I'm not a child. Kiss me."

He studied her as they treaded water. Had something horrible happened to her in college that she couldn't tell him about? "Did a boyfriend get to rough with you?"

"What?" She swallowed water when a small wave hit her. Coughing, she shook her head. "No boyfriend frightened me."

"That narrows it, somewhat."

"Look, Wakefield, if you're looking for an excuse not to kiss me, fine. See ya'."

When she would have flung herself away from him, he caught her arm, bringing her back to him, right up against his chest. "You're still a child, Bedelia."

"Nineteen is a woman. And I can't tread water forever."

He laughed harshly. "I'm a fool."

"I agree," she said, laughing too. Her hands cupped his face. "I'll sink if you don't hold me."

"I'll hold you." Dolph knew all his bridges had crumbled. For the first time in memory he didn't give a rap about his career or scripts or the future. Bedelia was now!

The kiss was gentle, searching. When Bedelia's lips parted readily, he thought his heart would burst from his chest.

They sank into the water, their mouths moving on each other, their bodies pressed tight together.

Surfacing, they swallowed great gulps of air.

Dolph studied her for long moments. Her eyes were wide and like turquoise pansies. Her lips trembled. She feathered her hands over him as though she'd forgotten they were a quarter mile out in the sea.

"Not here," he said brusquely.

"Good idea. Don't go all tight and cold on me

on the swim back, Wakefield." She wanted him with a basic, earthy need. If some day all she had were memories, she wanted the intimacy so that it could live in her heart forever.

"I'm not at all cold, Bedelia."

They swam back quickly, their bodies touching. Though their strokes were strong and sure, friction built with every contact. Dolph was amazed the water didn't boil.

Never had his senses been so sharpened. He felt as though he'd touched the pulse of the planet.

Bedelia was shaken and excited. Her body quivered with an awareness that was new to her. Though she'd had male friends for years, some of them important, her reactions to them weren't even close to the cascade, the hurricane, that Dolph Wakefield engendered in her.

Reaching the beach, Dolph swung her up into his arms, carrying her to the car.

She twined her arms around his neck. "Why aren't you looking at me?" Fear that he didn't really want her stabbed through her excitement. At that moment she couldn't have borne it if his desire didn't match hers.

"Bedelia, you call the shots. You owe me nothing. There are no bonds holding you to me. You are free to walk away at any time. And you can stay in my house as long as you want. You can say no to me at any time or all the time. You will never be pressured by word or gesture. Do you understand me? I want you . . . but more than that, I want you free and unafraid."

"I told you I'm not a child, and my comprehension is very good. In fact, I had a three-point-eight grade average when . . ." She pushed her face into his neck. No need to tell him that Orton had pressured her so much and so constantly to give him money that she'd been relieved to go along with a friend's suggestion to drop out and do a bike tour of Europe. Orton would be hard-pressed to find her on the itinerary she'd followed. But she'd bet he was trying to find her. Damn him. Why didn't he take no for an answer?

"Again you don't want to talk about it." Dolph tightened his hold, wondering at the pain that assailed him. Privacy was something he respected. His need to know everything about Bedelia transcended that.

"Right." She blew in his ear. "Just trying to keep you warm until we get to our destination." Once more, excitement curled in her. She felt no trepidation about the immediate future, and that surprised her.

"There's no problem with keeping warm," he said, "but please don't stop what you're doing. It's wonderful. As he set her on her feet next to the car, he looked at her for the first time. Her open smile coursed over him like a shivery caress. "We're going back to the house. Lorette will have left us a supper since she won't be returning until morning."

"We'll be alone."

"Yes." He closed her door, then got in the driver's side. "We'll be alone." She was so beautiful, he thought, so other-worldly, so delightful.

"I can handle that, Wakefield. Can you? Hey, is that a smile on your face?" She lifted her hand to his ear, tracing its curve with one finger. Being free to touch him was a warm triumph.

"You're outrageous, brat, but yes, it's a smile on my face . . . and I do think I can handle it." Heart pounding, he started the car and pulled out of the parking area.

"I know you can get this heap going faster than this. I've been with you when you have."

"I'm widening your options," he said softly.

Shifting closer to him, she put her foot over his on the accelerator pedal, pressing hard.

The car jumped like a wild thing. He should have stopped her, told her to remove her foot for safety's sake, but he didn't. The feel of her bare foot over his was so damned erotic, he reeled with the sensation. He was sure he'd never experienced such heady sexuality, and he wanted it to continue.

She wriggled her toes. "I like your foot."

"I like yours."

"The mating of the feet. How . . . stimulating," she said sweetly.

"Siren." He jerked to a stop in front of the villa. They both got out, and he joined her on her side of the car. "There will always be time to change your mind."

"I'm not giving you the same option," she said, her smile impish.

He closed the door of the car and pulled her into his arms. His kiss was gentle but urgent, his arms tight around her. His blood seemed to boil through his veins. "Bedelia," he said softly, wonderment in his voice, "I hope you're a witch. No human should have such power."

She laughed and clung to him when he lifted her into his arms, her fingers combing through his hair.

Striding into the house, he passed through the kitchen to the large sun-room.

"Are we going into the hot tub?" she asked.

"Too warm for that, but we can take a shower together. The one out here is large enough for two."

She nuzzled her face in his neck, nibbling at the taut skin there. "That sounds nifty."

"Bedelia," he said evenly, "I'd rather you didn't do that until after we shower."

"Gets to you?"

"It gets to me."

"I find it pretty sexy myself."

Dolph walked into the tiled room and switched on the faucets while still holding her. When she started to push down one strap of her bathing suit, he looked at her, a tight, sweet smile on his face. "No, let me take off your suit, please."

Shivering, she nodded. "I don't want you to think I'm scared because I'm shaking. I'm not. I'm just excited."

"So am I."

When he knelt in front of her, Bedelia held his head between her hands. "My heart's pounding something fierce. If you're giving me a heart attack, Wakefield, I'll sue."

"Then I'd better get ready to do the same. My heart's pounding too." Rolling the wet suit down her body was wonderfully erotic. He couldn't stop the trembling of his hands and was almost deafened by the blood roaring in his head.

Her breasts were perfection. Not large, but pert and uptilted. The nipples were a deep pink, and he had to take one in his mouth and caress it.

"Oh . . . oh," she gasped. "I'm melting . . . I think."

"So am I, Bedelia, darling. So am I." His mouth roved her abdomen hungrily, touching every pore.

Then he pulled the suit completely off her, lifting each foot and kissing it as he did so.

Her hands clenched convulsively in his hair. "I . . . think you've . . . done this before. You're very good at it."

"No."

"No what?"

"No, I never done precisely this with anyone else, but I hope I'm good at it. I want to make you happy."

"You're off to a good start." She sighed as they stepped into the shower.

With slow, gentle caresses they laved each other, sudsing away the salt bloom, shampooing their hair, touching, clinging. Then they dried each other in leisurely strokes.

Dolph stared at her as she stood in front of him. She wasn't self-conscious, but there was a measure of shyness. "Does it bother you that I love to look at your body?"

"No-o-o, but I can't say I'm used to the scrutiny." She traced his lips with one finger. "Are we going to stay in the sun-room?"

"Only if you'd like. I thought you might prefer my bedroom."

She nodded.

Hand in hand they strolled from the room, both naked and comfortable.

Dolph squeezed her hand when they entered his large bedroom. "Well, what do you think?"

She stared at the round bed against the far wall. "Good Lord, they really make beds like that? I thought it was just in the movies. What are we going to do? Box the compass?"

He shouted with laughter. "Bedelia Fronsby! Where did you get that expression?"

"A book, maybe. Or a movie. I don't recall. Is it bad?"

"Provocative. Making love in every direction of the compass might prove to be an all-night effort . . . and more."

"I'm game."

He was still laughing when he swept her up into his arms, his mouth plundering hers. Sexual excitement such as he'd never dreamed of was only heightened by the humor. "How can you make me feel so sexy and amuse me at the same time?"

"I come from a family of clowns?"

"Do you?" He felt her withdrawal, saw the shadows in her eyes. "Tell me."

Bedelia shook her head. What was there to tell? That she had a stepbrother whose whole purpose in life seemed to be to drive her crazy? That she feared him, not because of how he'd hurt her in the past, but because she was scared of the permanent damage he'd do to her attitude toward men? She'd always avoided Orton at all turns, but since meeting Dolph, she'd become convinced that she had to face Orton down on every issue, stand up for herself, assert her rights. And she could do that!

It was a Victorian tale at best, she thought. Better not to dwell on it, especially with Dolph holding her. Besides, the less she thought about Orton, the less she disliked him.

Placing her on the bed, Dolph touched her face. "Can I bring your focus back to me?"

"Easily." She cupped her hand to his cheek. "You're in my mind most of the time anyway."

Her simple candor rocked him, and he pressed his face to her breasts, his tongue sweeping along the inner curves. Then he lifted his head, tamping down his passion. There was something he had to say to her. "Bedelia, it might help to tell me, or anyone, about whatever it is that disturbs you so much."

"If it were a big thing, I'd tell you. But it's more irritating than anything else. And some of it is more what I envision than what really happened. I find the subject distasteful." She kissed him. "Now is not the time for it."

Fine thing, she mused, to tell Dolph that one of the reasons she was on the run in Europe was to keep her stepbrother from hitting her up for any more loans and telling her she should marry him for her own protection. That gave her the shivers. And there just wasn't enough of the small annuity she'd inherited to carry two people. Orton wanted the insurance money too, but that wasn't going to happen. She would need that to start her business one day. Until then she'd stay out of his way.

Lifting Dolph's face, she stared at him. "I want

to think of you, of us, and of what we're doing, not of what's in another world." She feathered her fingers over his neck and shoulders, shoving Orton to the back porch of her mind. "Did I tell you that I think you're a hunk, Wakefield?"

Laughter rolled out of him. "And you're a sexy wench, Bedelia."

"Really? I've always wanted to be a pirate's wench. You know, big boobs spilling out of a lacy bertha, hair down to my coccyx, and a permanent tear in my eye and tremble on my lip. *Wunderbar.*" Was she talking to much? Did her nervousness show through the desire?

Again amazed that he could laugh and still feel sexy, Dolph kissed her. "Do you speak German?"

"Enough to get me in and out of Bonn. Never mind the atlas questions. I want to be a wench and you can be a pirate. But, Wakefield, you don't have those high boots that flop over."

He pushed his face between her breasts, blowing gently. "Next time." Cupping one breast, he sucked it, then worried the nipple with his teeth. "Umm, you're so delicious."

"Heavens, I didn't . . . know . . . you . . . were a cannibal. I'm on fire." Surprise laced her voice as she wriggled closer to him, loving his touch.

"So am I."

Giving, taking, and sharing, they touched and embraced, kissed and held, explored and loved.

When Bedelia thought she would explode with a nameless want, when the heat inside her fanned to white, she groaned his name.

Dolph felt his own being explode as he positioned himself over her and started to enter. Feeling her sudden rigidity, he pulled back. "Bedelia, look at me. Look at me."

"Now is not the time for conversation." She tried to tug his mouth back to hers.

"Are you a virgin?"

"What difference does it make? Just know I'm not the campus groupie."

"You are a virgin."

"Dolph Wakefield!" she wailed. "You pick the damnedest time to do a questionnaire. It makes no difference."

"But it does, my little one. Don't look like that. I'm not going to stop."

"You'd better not." Dolph had to be the one, she thought in a sensual daze. He was the only man she'd ever wanted to touch her.

He chuckled, his mouth scoring over her breasts and abdomen.

Her whole body tingling in joyous reaction, Bedelia made soft little sounds in her throat. Heaven was gentle bites made by a movie actor named Dolph Wakefield. In her nineteen years she hadn't felt so unfettered, so free. At the same time she sensed that Dolph had roped her to him, holding her in unbreakable strands.

His hands were tender but questing. They teased her, as did his mouth. Little by little she became even more pliant beneath him.

Her body seemed to glide to his, to slide to him naturally. Hot and hotter, she felt she'd really turned to boiling honey. "Dolph," she murmured.

"Yes, my sweet one, I'm here. I want you. Do you want me?"

"I want something desperately, but you keep backing away, teasing me."

He lifted his head, and she saw his eyes were heavy with the passion he was restraining. He smiled. "I want your first time to be perfect."

She touched his cheek. "I expect discomfort. I know enough about it, even though before now I was never eager to experiment."

"Don't expect pain, my love." He lowered his head to her body once more.

When his lips and tongue swept over her thighs, she stiffened and tried to pull back.

"No, darling, I'm loving you."

"But—"

"Shhh, Bedelia. Feel the power." His tongue touched her most intimately, then intruded more deeply.

Her body arched; she couldn't mask the small scream. Then fires washed over her in a rhythm that matched his touch. Her head thrashed on the pillow. Her breathing was rough. Every pore on her skin pulsated with new blood.

Dolph felt her sexual ascension, the mounting pressure and excitement. She gasped, her body bucking beneath him. As she was slipping over the edge, he moved up and into her, feeling the breaking of the membrane even as his passion spiraled out of control. "Yes, yes, darling," he murmured. "Let go. I have you."

Her fingers dug into him, her nails scoring down his back, as she called out to him, chaining him to her.

They crested together, reaching the ultimate in physical love, bound in passion—giving, giving. Release!

Bodies slick with love dew they held each other, limbs entwined, still together. Without words they'd committed and given all.

Awed, Bedelia looked at him, panting, wide-eyed. "I've climbed Everest . . . and fallen off."

"And you took me with you, darling." He winced as she shifted slightly. He loved being part of her.

"Do we have to get up, ever?" she asked, yawning. Then her mouth snapped shut. "That's not supposed to happen."

"What?" he asked lazily, his face nestled into her neck. He grunted in pleasure when their bodies separated. He loved her.

"I'm not supposed to . . . you know, do that, have that feeling when I make love the first time. It isn't done. It's biologically impossible or something. It can't happen. I'm not sore." She gazed up at him. "Did we do it wrong?"

"We did it so right, we may have to put our relationship in the Smithsonian."

Grinning, she kissed his nipples. "Well, I guess we could do that, but it's awfully public, Wakefield."

"We'll find a quiet reading room."

"Done." She cuddled even closer. "Don't leave me."

"I have no intention of doing that."

After a moment of silence, he opened one eye and glanced down at her. "I've decided. Forget the Smithsonian. No way will we be doing that in public, my sweet. Will you stay with me?" The question hung out there as though all the joy of the world hinged on it. It did!

"How long?" Did he want her just for tomorrow? she wondered. His answer could make or break her.

"As long as you can." He loosed a shaky breath. "I want you to finish your education, but I want us to be together. Can we do that?" He wanted to make a commitment to her, cherish her, care for her.

Blushing with delight, she nodded. "I don't want to leave you." Her smile wobbled. "Won't you get tired of the gauche one when you're with so many sophisticated women of the world?"

He pulled her down to him, kissing her deeply. "What we just shared was unique and beautiful. I'll want it always." He smiled at her. "I'll see many beautiful, intelligent women in my work, and in my work I'll pretend to make passionate love to them. But there's only you, Bedelia, in my mind and soul." Maybe it was too soon to tell her that, but conviction overrode caution.

She rested her head on his chest. "I can't believe we're saying this to each other, that we're lovers. It's great." She kissed his chest, sighing. "It's as though we lifted a veil and enclosed ourselves in our own private world. I love it."

"I love you." With that declaration Dolph released all the bonds around his being and gave himself to her. The ice in his soul melted. There was only Bedelia and the heat and life she gave him.

"I love you too, Dolph. And it was easy. I

thought I could never love anybody without knowing him for a hundred years, without knowing every facet of his personality."

"We'll learn everything about each other . . . slowly, savoring the revelations." His hand whorled over her bare back, edging her closer. He kissed her long and deeply, his body hardening.

"Heavens, Wakefield, are you Superman or something? I didn't think we could do it again so soon." She laughed down at him, very comfortably lying atop him.

He stiffened. "Are you sore? Would you rather not?"

"I'm not sore," she said, holding him fast when he would have moved from under her. "I'd just heard that it couldn't be done so quickly . . . if you know what I mean." She smiled shyly.

He chuckled. "To tell you the truth, it's a new one on me, love. It's just your power." He kissed her again.

"Umm, wonderful." She gave herself over to the carousel of desire, swinging, swaying, twirling in joy.

Passion took them like a wild storm. Hungry for each other, they gave and gave. And in the giving, they took it all. Life was an incandescent, brilliant kaleidoscope just for them.

"Not ever did I expect this, Bedelia, love," Dolph murmured when they once more lay satiated and exhausted.

"Then you can guess how surprised I am."

All through the night they held each other, loving, sleeping, waking to love again.

When Dolph had to go to work the next day, they stood in the drive kissing, loath to let go.

"Hurry home," Bedelia said at last.

"I will." It took all his self-control to drive away.

Three

The days turned into weeks, and Dolph was stunned by the happiness he felt. Sometimes he'd look at Bedelia and wonder if she would change toward him. She was young. There was much she hadn't experienced. That thought was a knife cut. He knew a person's tastes could change radically through the early twenties. At twenty-nine, he was nearer thirty than twenty, and more settled.

Bedelia forgot about her stepbrother, about all the vagaries and annoyances in her past. For the first time in her life she thought of roots, ties, commitment. Dolph filled her days and nights. When he was away from her, she suffered gray moods, sure he'd tire of her. When he was with her, he was all the sunshine and moonlight she'd ever need. Whenever she worried about how long it would be before he'd want someone else, she fought her fears, struggling to banish them from her mind.

Happiness built and expanded every day. The closer Dolph and Bedelia became, the more life and the fates seemed to smile on them. All the bricks of their different personalities fit, and the mortar was their love. Nothing could cloud the sweetness of their time together. No one would be allowed into their world.

They swam and sailed, sailboarded and walked, always together, hands and bodies touching. At Dolph's urging Bedelia contacted UCLA and was gratified by their positive response. She could enroll and transfer her credits.

Dolph could tell the picture was going well. The director was smiling most days, and had even complimented Dolph on his work. Still, Dolph was eager for the filming to be done. He couldn't help imagining the future, Bedelia with him in California. He'd be working. She'd get her degree and begin whatever career she chose. Maybe wife and mother could be part of that.

His blood thudded faster at the thought. Marriage kept popping into his mind, but he told himself not to broach the subject until she got her education. She needed the freedom to concentrate on her work and decide what she wanted out of life.

Every day was Sunday for Bedelia. As well as working in the garden, she also helped Lorette when she could and boned up on her French. She wanted to resume study of the language when she started at UCLA.

"You bloom like the rose, mademoiselle," Lorette said one day when she came out into the garden to gather some herbs. "And it is good to hear you singing."

Bedelia grinned at the housekeeper. "I'm happy."

"I can see that for myself. M'sieur is the cause, *hein?*"

"*Oui.*" Bedelia laughed out loud.

Life was so rich and joyous, Dolph believed he would never be unhappy again. Yet one afternoon, after he had finished a difficult scene, the most crucial one before the cast and crew flew back to the United States, he found two men waiting for him.

"I'm Orton Bledsoe," one of them said. He was a heavy-set man, already balding, although he looked little more than thirty years old. "I am Bedelia Fronsby's legal guardian. This is my lawyer, M'sieur Demond." He glared at Dolph. "You tried to hide my sister from me."

"This is an injunction, m'sieur." Demond handed Dolph a folded paper, then frowned at Bledsoe.

Dolph stared at the injunction, his mind working. Was this the glitch in Bedelia's life? Why was the name Orton familiar? "Explain," he said to the lawyer.

"The law protects persons like Bedelia, Mr. Wakefield," Bledsoe answered. "You actors may think you're above the law, but you're not."

"I've never pretended to be," Dolph said quietly, eyeing the belligerent Bledsoe. Why was he there? Dolph had the sure instinct that it wasn't to protect Bedelia. "What do you want?" He noted how the other man blinked at the sudden query.

"M'sieur Bledsoe means—" the lawyer began.

"I can do my own talking, Demond. This injunction says that you stay away from my sister, Wakefield."

Dolph read through the paper. "If I read this right, Bedelia is your stepsister, Bledsoe." He kept his tone soft, but there was an edge of steel to it.

"Whatever." Bledsoe's chin jutted out. "You will not see Bedelia again. According to my stepfather's will, Bedelia is under my guardianship—"

"I'll want to read a copy of that. So will my lawyers," Dolph said abruptly. "The way I see it, you don't have a legal leg to stand on, Bledsoe." He flung the paper at him.

M. Demond rolled his eyes as though he might agree with that.

"Don't try to steamroll me." Bledsoe's voice rose, taking on a whining tone. "Stay away from Bedelia. You're not going to make her into your whore—"

Dolph dropped him with a blow flush to the jaw. He looked down at the man. "Don't ever," he told Bledsoe, spread-eagled on the floor, "use that word in connection with Bedelia."

"I'll—I'll sue!" Bledsoe shouted, pushing himself up.

Dolph had already spun on his heel and was striding away.

That evening he told Bedelia what had happened.

She nodded. "Orton and Demond were here. He's trying to make me go back to New York with him. He's been hunting for me all this time, but I won't go." She threw herself into Dolph's arms. "I love you."

"And I love you, my sweet thing."

"Then marry me, and he can't touch me."

"Oh God, Bedelia, I want to, more than you can ever know. But you're so young."

"I want us to be together."

"Oh, baby, so do I." He kissed her, lifting her feet off the floor, their mouths clinging.

The feel of his hot skin set Bedelia on fire. Passion was always just beneath the surface. Now it exploded between them.

As Dolph's mouth scored down her cheek to her neck, she doffed her light halter dress, letting it pool around her feet.

Dolph stripped quickly too, his mouth never leaving her. His lips slid down to her breasts, worshiping one, then the other, in slow, sweet desire. He slipped one hand between them, touching the cluster of curls at the junction of her legs. His fingers eased inside her, quivering, teasing, making her wet and wild. "Darling. Bedelia."

"Dolph." She sighed in trembling joy, tensing against him when his fingers began a melody inside her. Hot bliss built within her, and she twisted and turned, desperate for satisfaction.

Watching her face, he stroked the sensitive nub, chanting her name in rhythm with his wanton fingers. When she struggled against him, trying to move back so she could caress him too, he held her fast.

"I'm too hot for you, love," he whispered.

They kissed—ravenous, needy. He sucked on her tongue. She shivered with joy.

"I want you," she half groaned in his ear.

"I love you, Bedelia."

He lifted her up his body, then let her slide back down until she fitted over his arousal. Her gasp was all the impetus he needed.

They took each other in wild love, tied together in everlasting threads.

When the scandal broke in the French and English tabloids, Bedelia knew Dolph's career was damaged, maybe irreparably. He denied it.

She could recall vividly the many conversations they'd had about careers, choices . . . and hopes. Dolph loved what he did. His eyes glittered with animation and life when he talked about film-making, acting and directing. Bedelia had no doubt his work was vitally important to him. It shouldn't be taken away because of something in his personal life, but the public and his profession were capricious. There was no way to gauge what the reaction would be. Someone could shoot to the moon on notoriety, while another person fell into an anonymous pit, never to rise again.

Like a dog with a bone, Bedelia worried all the options in her brain. With each new tawdry article, she became more depressed.

DOLPH WAKEFIELD, RISING AMERICAN CINEMA STAR, KEEPS UNDERAGE GIRL AS HIS PERSONAL LOLITA

"I'm not Lolita," she exclaimed to Dolph a week after the first tabloid report. "I'm much older. I've been on my own, paying my own bills, and I'm not underage. Why don't they print that?" She buried her face in his chest.

He hugged her. "Shh, it'll die down, I'm sure of it. We leave for the States in a few days, and that'll be the end of it." That Bedelia was deeply affected by the news stories was obvious to him. More than once he'd caught her with her fist pressed to her mouth, shaking her head slowly. When he questioned her, she tried to smile and slough it off.

"Yes, you're right," she said. "Let's leave as fast as we can." In Dolph's arms she felt safe. She closed her eyes and pressed tighter to him. She wouldn't think of Orton and his dogged malice that had been her bête noir for much of her childhood.

Dolph loved her. She loved him. They'd marry. Everything would be fine.

Nothing would have gotten her from Dolph's side—except a visit from Orton the next day.

Orton didn't waste time on niceties. "Do you think," he asked nastily, "that you can live irresponsibly forever? You don't come into the bulk of your inheritance for two more years. That's the way the will reads. And I can petition the court to be your guardian if your behavior continues along its erratic course."

"All you ever talk about is the money, Orton." She was annoyed that he'd come back to see her after she'd told him never to return to the villa. "You've tried to get at my annuity more than once." She smiled when he scowled. "And you won't get it. The insurance money and the rest of my legacy are sewed up tight, Orton."

"The only reason I approached old Brooks for a loan was to cover an investment I'd made for the both of us." He frowned at her. "Besides, I said I'd marry you."

"I don't want that, or your investments, or any discussion on it. I'm old enough to make up my own mind and, when the time comes, handle my money. I will stay with Dolph."

Orton watched her closely. "You're wrecking his career."

"No, I'm not. Dolph said I wasn't."

"Did he? Then all the gossip about him losing the lead in *Wanderlust* is wrong? I don't think so. How about the plum part in *Easy Man*? He lost that too."

"That's not true," she said shakily.

"Yes, it is. Why don't you call his agent and ask him? Or better yet, read the trades. Your lover's career is going down the tubes. Look at this." He shoved an Italian and a French tabloid at her.

Though she wasn't an expert in either language, she could make out enough to know that they agreed pretty much with Orton's assessment.

That night, when she faced Dolph with them, he shrugged them off. "Those parts were sought by many other able people, Bedelia. People who are hardworking and talented. The competition was hot. That's why I didn't get either part, not because of what the tabloids said."

She wanted to believe that with all her heart. But Orton's words spun around in her head. When she read an American article, its tone slicing through Dolph's work and reputation like a rapier, she called Orton.

"You're smart to get out of there, Bedelia," her stepbrother said patronizingly.

"Just stay out of my way, Orton. I don't want you anywhere near me."

"But—"

"I mean that. I'll take action against you if I must. Good-bye."

That night in bed, she embraced and caressed Dolph greedily.

"Darling! I love it." He kissed her, his joy with her obvious. "I love you."

"I love you, Dolph." In fevered giving, she moved down his body, loving him the way he'd always loved her. Gently, she took him into her mouth. His sighs, groans, and gasping of her name telegraphed his monumental pleasure.

"Darling, darling! Bedelia. My God, I'm yours."

Caught in the whirlwind, they loved and gave until they were one person.

The next day, before Dolph left for a reshooting, she kissed him over and over again.

His smile was lopsided when he put her away from him, his eyes warm with passion and love. "We leave in two days, darling. Then we'll be together in sunny California."

"Good-bye, Dolph. Have a nice day." What a banal remark for a tearing, wrenching parting.

She wrote a note and put it on his pillow. She didn't even say good-bye to Lorette, but waited until the other woman had gone to the market. Then she left, borrowing a bicycle to get from the villa into the village. There she hopped a bus to the airport in Nice. She bought a ticket and didn't use it. In the rest room, she hid her hair under a French cap, dressed in jeans and an Oxford cotton shirt, then left for the train station, boarding the TGV to Paris as a young man.

Four

Summer had faded into autumn, and the Manhattan air had a crisp feel to it, though it was still relatively warm. Striding along Seventh Avenue toward the Greenwich Village restaurant where he was to meet his agent, Dolph inhaled deeply. The unusually fresh air cleared his head somewhat, still foggy from a night of script reading. Although he was late for the breakfast meeting, he knew the brisk walk would do him good. Once he'd finally gotten to bed the previous night, his sleep had been disturbed by familiar dreams of Bedelia. The dreams had grown blessedly infrequent over the more than ten years since he'd last seen her, but they still had the power to cast him into a blue funk. And he didn't need that today. The lunch meeting was with new backers for a movie he wanted to direct.

When Dolph at last reached the restaurant, his agent was pacing in front of it.

"Hi, Marion," Dolph greeted him.

His agent gave him a long-suffering look. Only Dolph called him that. He didn't particularly like his first name and always referred to himself as Welmer. "Where have you been? Our breakfast meeting has been changed to the new backer's offices."

Dolph frowned. "What the hell? Who are these people anyway?" He wasn't in the mood for arbitrary behavior.

"Now, don't get upset," Welmer said placatingly, hurrying his client toward the car waiting for them.

Dolph frowned at Welmer. "I don't like this shuffling around, and I'll tell them that."

Welmer rolled his eyes, but he said no more as he followed Dolph into the car.

The driver drove them down toward the lower tip of Manhattan, letting them off in front of a towering edifice that loomed into the sky like a shiny glass harmonica.

Welmer took Dolph's arm, urging him into the building. "They have the top three floors. We're to take the elevator at the back." When Dolph hesitated, Welmer stopped. "Relax, Dolph. I know you have a tough schedule right now, trying to wrap up your latest picture, but this is a plum contract. You did say you wanted to do this."

Dolph shifted, flexing his arms as though he carried a heavy burden. Why was he so jumpy? "I did say that," he agreed. "Let's go."

In a minute they were in an elevator, speeding to the executive floor of Delia Cosmetics International.

Still feeling edgy, Dolph stalked through the outer office, giving his name to a dumbfounded secretary. She quickly rose and opened double doors to an inner office. With Welmer at his heels, Dolph strode into the room.

"Ah, there she is," Welmer said, moving around Dolph. He gestured toward a woman silhouetted against the floor-to-ceiling windows. Sunlight made an aureole around her. "Delia, I'd like you to meet Dolph Wakefield. Dolph, this is Delia of Delia Cosmetics International."

She walked out of the sunlight and Dolph saw her. It was like being blindsided! "Bedelia!" She'd been in his mind so much, for a moment he was sure he was hallucinating. Planets and stars swirled in his head. All breath left him. She was here! In Manhattan! Not in Nice, but right in front of him!

"Dolph?" Welmer asked, concerned. "What's the matter?"

"Nothing." He stared at her, and she met his gaze steadily.

Bedelia had been prepared to see him. Since the day she left him, she had followed his career for years like the most devout fan. She'd written him countless letters, only to tear them up. Once, when he'd been filming in Paris, she'd even called him.

So, yes, she'd readied herself for the meeting. But she hadn't expected the cosmic explosion in her being when he'd looked at her. Dolph still had the power. Her palms were damp, her insides trembling, but she held herself up straight and motionless.

"Say something, Dolph," Welmer muttered from the side of his mouth, his glances shooting from one to the other.

"Yes, say something, Dolph." Bedelia tried her professional smile, but it wouldn't come together. "It's been a long time."

"You know each other?" Welmer asked, astonished.

"Miss Bedelia Fronsby and I met many years ago," Dolph said harshly, "when she was still . . . a child." She was facing him, he realized, still stunned. The waif. No. The sleek, sophisticated, beautiful creature. Bedelia!

"Nineteen is not a child, Dolph," she said. "And I'm called Delia now." Perspiration beaded her upper lip. He'd disconcerted her so easily, yet he'd been shocked to see her. She was sure of it. He was so damned cool. Digging her fingernails into her hands, she struggled for composure.

"Will the meeting be here?" Welmer asked, again glancing between the two of them.

"No," Bedelia said tartly. "In the boardroom. Over there."

Welmer nodded, then scurried across the room and through the open door, pulling it shut behind him.

Silence. Like contenders in a ring waiting for the bell, they sized each other up.

"How are you, Dolph?" He was perfect, she thought. Too handsome, too healthy, too in control. He'd always been more of everything than anyone else, and his sensual power could set off a charge that would flatten the Côte d'Azur.

"Fine," he answered. She was as slim and tall

as ever, he mused, but where there'd been open-
ness, guilelessness, and laughter, there was now
containment, a touch-me-not aura. She was inor-
dinately beautiful. That gamine face was much
the same, but the cheekbones seemed wider, the
chin firmer. Had all of her softness turned to
tanned leather?

Her makeup was flawless, nearly invisible. The
coral-colored raw silk dress was obviously French,
haute couture. Her hair was still auburn fire, the
eyes that wonderful turquoise that changed from
green to blue, depending on her mood. When she
was passionate, they were a fiery green.

"So you're Delia Cosmetics?"

"Yes. And on my own, without my stepbrother
. . . most of the time."

Dolph inclined his head. "How did you manage
that?"

"Diligence."

He stiffened with pain when her dimples flashed,
her lips lifting in a fleeting, remembered smile.

"So, welcome to our corporate headquarters,"
she said. "You're almost prompt." Had he grown,
she wondered, and taken on a greater masculine
beauty? Dolph had always been sexy. Now he
exuded a virility that had her blinking.

"And quite a place it is. I'm impressed. I expect
that was the reason for switching breakfast from
a mere restaurant." He eyed her from heel to toe.
It gave him black satisfaction to see the run of
blood up her neck. The lift of her chin was a
familiar gesture.

"Sometimes we try to impress our clients,
Dolph. But, in essence, don't you work for us?"

Her words didn't mask her irritation. When had he become so pompous?

"I had no idea we would be contracting with you, Bedelia. How did you get your hands on *Southwind*?" Did she know the part could've been tailor-made for him? he wondered. Damn her.

Bedelia stiffened at his caustic tone. "Our company has been known to make good buys and investments." When Dolph's satiric smile widened, she had to suppress a shiver.

"I've always liked a winner."

His gentle tone didn't fool her for a minute. "Then you'll enjoy working for us." She tore her gaze from him and glanced at the boardroom door. "Shall we join the others? It's this way."

Dolph followed her, his gaze running up her svelte figure. The silk of her dress whispered against her and delineated every sweet curve of her body.

As if she could feel his scrutiny, Bedelia stiffened her spine. She felt caught . . . and touched. His very breathing imprisoned her. He took the air from her lungs.

In the boardroom, introductions were made between her lawyer and business advisor and his. As she walked to the head of the table, she felt him still at her back. She took deep breaths to get back on keel. Yet when he held her chair for her, every fine hair on her body lifted.

Dolph answered when spoken to, accepted one of the flaky croissants that was offered, ate some of the fresh pineapple. He drank several cups of black coffee. Though he looked at others, he saw only Bedelia.

Bedelia ate a little fruit, drank some papaya juice, and spoke to everyone but Dolph.

After nearly two hours, the meeting was at last winding down, the lawyers haggling over a couple of sticky points. Bedelia and Dolph were completely silent, looking only at each other.

Finally the meeting was over. Everyone shook hands and dispersed, one by one. Welmer hesitated by Dolph's chair, obviously baffled by his client's lack of interest in the proceedings. He touched Dolph's arm.

"What?" Dolph looked at Welmer as though they'd never met.

"Do you want me to drop you somewhere?"

"No, thanks, Marion. I'll walk. I need the fresh air."

Welmer nodded, frowning. "You're not going to do anything foolish that might quash the deal, are you, Dolph?" A smile flitted across his face. His nervous laugh turned into a cough when Dolph stared stonily at him. "Of course you're not." Dolph looked away, and Welmer shrugged and followed the others out the door.

When only he, Bedelia, and her secretary were left in the room, Dolph turned to Bedelia.

"Tell her to leave," he said bluntly. "I want to speak to you, privately. And you know that."

Before her astonished secretary could say anything, Bedelia put her hand on her arm. "Better get in touch with Harolds, Lydia."

Lydia blinked at her boss, glanced at Dolph, then went out the door, leaving it open.

Dolph strode across the room and shut the door with a resounding slam. As he faced Bedelia again, silence stretched out between them, taut, zinging with tension, at the breaking point.

Suddenly he smacked the tabletop, then stalked to the belled window overlooking lower Manhattan and the harbor. "Why?"

Bedelia didn't pretend to misunderstand. "You were going to be bad-mouthed out of several good parts by the tabloids. And you know they can cause great damage, so don't deny it. You were on your way up, but you weren't in solid. Anything that besmirched you or was off-color could've sent your career into limbo for a long time, or even damaged it permanently." She inhaled a shuddering breath. "And there might have been some very hairy moments with my stepbrother and the legal procedures he could have brought to bear. I needed an education in order to stand on my own. I didn't want to be badgered by Orton. There were too many things against us."

Her chin up, she gazed beyond him. It still made her reel to be so close to him. For years all she'd had were newspaper blurbs and the occasional television picture. Of course she'd seen all of his movies. When he'd filmed in Paris, she'd gone every day, donning a dark scarf and sunglasses, getting as close to the shooting as she could. She'd seen him only from a distance, but she could still recall the pain, how she'd wanted to call to him. But she hadn't.

"I see," he said flatly. "And you didn't think I could handle my career, that bloody-minded stepbrother of yours, and your education?" Fury smoked out of him. How had she dared to dictate their lives in such an abitrary, poorly thought-out way!

"Most of it wasn't your business." Irritation began to simmer in her. Where did he get off being so high and mighty? He wasn't Zeus, for corn's sake. "Besides, your perception was different from mine. You had a great deal more to lose."

He whirled to face her. His mouth was twisted, his eyes glittering. "And I lost a great deal."

"So did I," she whispered.

They stared at each other for long moments, the duel silent, angry, frustrated. Their weapons were feelings that could slice through the other. Words were potential bombs. The air pulsed with years of hurt and loss, with accusations unvoiced.

Bedelia cleared her throat. "But I gained a good bit too. As you did."

His hands flexed at his sides. "You still have all the answers, don't you? Well, that decision should have been made by both of us, not just you. I didn't need you manipulating me." All those damned wasted, lonely years, he thought, the heartwrenching pain, the never-ending wondering where she was and if she was all right.

Her lips tightened. "Think what you choose. We both gained a new life from what I did." Despite her words, all the doubts she'd had over the years surfaced with a vengeance. She shivered, regret tearing at her.

Dolph let his gaze rove over her slowly. Her body was wonderfully curved. She couldn't be a pound heavier, but she'd gone from slim girl to tantalizing woman. Her childish body had rounded into a wondrous sophistication. Desire shot through him, an elemental need that shook him. He struggled to hide it behind his anger. "Once you would have blushed if I'd stared at you. Now you don't even flinch."

"I told you I've come a long way, she said steadily, but his implication was like a thousand tiny needles piercing her. Those more than ten years could have been yesterday for all the change in him. Oh, there had been a subtle metamorphosis. His toughness had acquired a layer of steel; the maverick sense of humor was tinted with the satiric. There was a closed look to him, a cynical twist to his smile, a frigid hardness to his eyes. But . . . she let her gaze roam over him, as he'd done to her. Dolph was still a hunk, a heartbreaker. His build, if anything, was better, harder, firmer, and set her heart pounding.

"Like what you see?" he drawled.

"What woman wouldn't? You're an international heartthrob." She tried to imitate his light tone, but she found it hard to swallow. She'd been prepared to see him, meet him, talk to him. But she had forgotten how he could absorb all the oxygen from the air, leaving behind his personal mystique of sensuousness and excitement. Finally she swallowed again. "And what you have is marketable to me and my business." She knew her remark was provocative, knew it was like a match to dry kindling, but she needed to put the ball in his court, get off the defensive. Her chin lifted another fraction.

"And that's the reason for the contract?" He'd caught a flicker of unsureness in her look. Like a hungry shark he smelled blood and maneuvered for the *coup de mort*. "And you've followed my career?"

She nodded slowly. His silky voice was subtly menacing.

She'd played him like a trout on a line, he thought with fury and incredulity. She'd watched him, hour after hour, day after day, year after agonizing year. Had she laughed at his efforts to find her? "Where were you?"

She blinked, disconcerted by the abrupt question. "Paris. I attended a small school outside the city at first, then the Sorbonne." She was uncomfortable. His smile hadn't changed, but . . .

"And?"

As if a dam had cracked, the words poured through, spilling into the room. "At first I lived on one of those dark narrow streets on the Left Bank, in a *conciergerie*." She didn't tell him she had barely moved for days, caught in a fog of loneliness and despair. He'd been the only life in her soul. "Then I found work as a maid in a hotel. When I started classes, I used the name Delia Bennett, my mother's maiden name. I dyed my hair," she added quietly.

"What?" Fury coursed through him. That wonderful hair despoiled. "A complete masquerade. Is that it?" She hadn't wanted him to find her . . . ever.

"Something like that."

"I looked all over Europe, including Paris." Anger melted the frost in his soul, turning it to dry ice. Memories froze. She'd had no need of him, or anything he had. She'd come a long way . . . without him. He hated her at that moment. "I found your stepbrother," he said, his voice as cold as his thoughts, "but he didn't seem to know where you were." Dolph didn't mention that he'd bloodied Orton's nose and almost choked the life out of him.

Once, when he'd been in Paris filming, he'd gone to a dive on the *Rive Gauche,* drinking and itching for a fight. "Would it have hurt to call?"

"I did call—six, seven years ago. You were directing your first film in Paris, I left a message at your hotel, but you never called back." Dolph stiffened. Was she telling the truth? Had his imprisonment in hell been lengthened by an inept hotel operator or desk clerk? Bedelia went on. "I wanted us to be equals when we met again." It was what she had told herself for years, but it sounded thin and silly.

"Now we're no longer on different strata," he said. "Is that it?"

His gentle tone was more threatening than anything she'd ever heard. "That was my intention." Yes, they were on common ground, but with bullet-proof shields thrown up between them. "Perhaps you don't understand. . . ."

"I think I do. You set the stage and placed me on it. And now I'll react according to plan." The evidence of her callous manipulation made him want to put his fist through the wall.

She could feel his rage and, horrified, stared at his sweet smile. "Dolph, I don't think—"

He moved back to the table, staring across it at

her. "Yes. You have all the patina of success. The dress, the handmade shoes, the pearl brooch, the pearl studs in your ears. Well done. You've buried the street urchin completely."

Baffled, angered, she nodded. "Totally. Though I was never exactly destitute. I had an annuity from my father's will, and my parents' life insurance."

"I see."

"And you've come a long way from being a struggling actor." But he'd always seemed successful to her. And now he'd broadened and deepened . . . and turned cold.

Bedelia knew nothing about Dolph, and everything. He didn't like even one dot of grease on his pasta, and his salads had to be laden with juicy tomatoes and fresh-cut basil. He loved olives right from the brine, and fish broiled over an open fire. But she didn't know his family, his history. They'd skated over that. When they'd been together, all they'd wanted was each other. No other person was allowed.

Having read the trades, she now knew he'd been born to money and power. She knew about his closest friends, Piers Larraby and Bear Kenmore. In their own ways they were as famous as he. But what of Dolph himself? He'd been her lover and friend. She saw a different man in front of her now. Was her Dolph gone forever?

Studying him, she saw the infinitesimal shifting of his features and knew, with a flash of memory, he was on a new track. She didn't know which way it would take them . . . but the menace had diminished.

"So long, Bedelia," he said. Her mouth dropped

open, and she stared at him, dumbfounded, but he said no more. Spinning on his heel, he went to the door, opened it, then slammed it shut behind him.

"Dolph." Her whisper was loud in the stillness. There'd been so much more to say.

Once upon a time there'd been pulsing heat behind their every word, every nuance. This morning there'd been dry ice. Was it self-defense? The social jousting that people did when meeting after a long time? On the surface, the conversation could have been considered pleasant. So why did she feel as though she'd just made wild, passionate love . . . with a stranger?

Shaking her head, she returned to her office and tried to work. At eleven forty-five, frustrated by her inability to concentrate, she told Lydia she was taking an early lunch, though she was anything but hungry.

When she reached the street, she turned toward a nearby park. Walking with her head down, she edged around other pedestrians and crossed streets without noticing. The questions in her head, the image of Dolph, were the only reality.

After several blocks she slowed her pace. She had no answers, but the fresh air had helped. And it had stimulated some appetite. At the entrance to the park she paused in front of a hot-dog cart.

"Allow me."

She whirled to find Dolph standing directly behind her. He ordered two hot dogs, smeared them with relish and mustard, and held one out to her. "Here."

She took it, eyeing him warily. "Did you follow me?"

"Yes. Let's get some juice." He led her to a fresh-juice cart and ordered two. "Shall we find a bench?"

She nodded, not trusting her voice.

They sat down on a bench near a bike path and ate in silence. When they were through, Dolph asked her if she'd like some coffee.

"No," she said, "the juice is fine."

Silence.

Bedelia coughed. "I should get back. I've been gone longer than I meant to—"

"I'll walk you back to your office." He gathered up their rubbish and tossed it in a bin. When he took her arm as they walked out of the park, she didn't pull away.

"Will you have dinner with me tonight?" he asked. He had no intention of letting her out of sight for more than a few hours at a time if he could help it. Not until he had figured out the myriad emotions she aroused in him.

"I should invite you to eat at my place," she said. "You'd like the cook. I hired Lorette and brought her to America." Bedelia hurried her words, wanting the old time to come back, the old feelings, the camaraderie and kinship they'd had.

Dolph blinked, spun into the past. "Lorette? Why?" Stupid question! She'd pulled another rug out from under him.

"Why not?" Dolph at her table? she asked herself. It was absurd, bizarre. She'd told herself when she put her plan in motion that she'd expect no more than polite friendship from Dolph. Yet already she wanted so much more.

"Answering a question with a question?" he said. "All right, maybe next time we could eat at your place." He pressed her arm closer to him, so that their hips bumped gently as they walked. She was almost eye-level with him. "Still tall and leggy." He looked down. "Don't your feet hurt in those heels? As I recall, you were always more comfortable barefoot."

"I still am. But now my shoes don't hurt me." She grinned. "I can afford the ones that fit like a sneaker and look like a lethal weapon." It was their first snippet of true conversation, and she wanted to hug the moment to her. "I confess I usually wear sneakers to the park."

Her smile was potent, like the wine he'd tossed back the first night they met. His gaze traveled down her legs once more, lingering. He had the most overpowering desire to lead her back to the bench, take off her shoes, and kiss those feet. He remembered they were slender, long, and dainty, yet she'd had a swim kick that would have done credit to a world-class competitor.

He pulled himself free from his memories, fanning his anger once more. "They're handmade in Rome, no doubt."

Bedelia was uneasy. She could feel the tremors of rage emanating from him. "That was true. Now I've found a place in Little Italy, right here in Manhattan." She smiled again, but her insides were churning. She imagined this was how it felt to free-fall.

Dolph was quick. He would have figured out by

now that she'd been aware of him and where he was most of the time. He'd been far more visible than she over the years. That would eat at him like acid. . . .

Her heart thudded painfully at the thought of being rejected by him. She'd played that scenario in her mind many times, until she'd begun to believe she could handle it. But her very first sight of him had burst that bubble. Losing him a second time would be a deathblow.

She was snared anew by his magnetism, the power that could make her forget everything but him. But she was also wary of the very real anger she sensed in him. She quickened her pace. "I should get back to work."

Dolph didn't want to leave her. What if she disappeared again? He hated that fear. Bedelia had the capacity to unman him, to cripple him.

At that moment the plan was born. He could play the hidden game too. "So should I," he said. "I have a script to read."

Bedelia felt vulnerable, unsteady. Looking at him was like strolling on quicksand. She had a suspicion he was spinning a master plan. But what? Why?

A block from her office, he tugged her to a stop. "What made you buy into moviemaking?"

"An offer I couldn't refuse."

When she finally felt confident enough to meet him again, she'd decided to search for the perfect part for him, with the intention of backing the film. The one they'd just agreed on, *Southwind*, was the second one she'd found. She hadn't been able to touch the first one.

"We tried to purchase *Frozen Idol*," she said, "but that was all locked up." She looked at him. "You were great in it and deserved the Academy Awards you received for acting and directing. And now they even call you Frozen Idol in the trades, don't they?"

He nodded. "You know a lot about me, Bedelia."

"You're a celebrity." She tried to start walking again, but he kept a tight grip on her arm.

"You were DeLinde Company too?" he asked. "I remember they were the French company that was so eager to get a piece of *Idol*."

"Yes," she said, "but we only approached Mr. Belden, the author's agent, once. How did you find out about it?"

"We have the same agent. We talked."

"Oh. I see." But she didn't. "Do you know why Mr. Belden never wrote anything else?"

"He never said." Perhaps one day he'd tell her that Frank Belden was the pen name he'd used when he'd scripted *Frozen Idol* and that was why he'd accepted the Oscar on behalf of its "author."

"Oh," Bedelia said.

"DeLinde. You've had a lot of names, Bedelia."

She blinked. She was getting paranoid. He was smiling, his voice soft. Why had she shuddered? Silly. "That was my partner's name. I wish you could've met him. He was the most wonderful man."

Jealousy, like shards of green ice, stabbed through him. "How nice for you." There were tears in her eyes. Damn her! She'd loved the man.

"You would have liked him. He was so special," she said. She'd been heartbroken when Professor de Linde had died, just as their company had begun to pay off. She still missed the kindly older man who'd been like a father to her.

Impulsively Dolph leaned down and kissed the corner of her mouth. "For old times sake," he said hoarsely. He hated the tears she shed for the lost love; it wrenched him to see her crying.

He walked her the rest of the way to her office building and stopped in front.

"I'll meet you here about six and drive you home," he said.

"Fine." Bedelia couldn't seem to clear her throat. Her lips were on fire where he'd kissed her. Her memory of Professor de Linde was so sharp, yet nothing was clearer in her mind than Dolph. He'd kissed her! She had to bite her tongue hard to keep from sagging to the ground in boneless joy.

Dolph forewent the relative comfort of a cab. The day had turned from crisp to hot and humid, meant for riding, not striding. He was all but running. The Plan that had formed itself during the walk doused him like ice water. Bedelia was not getting away again, and he was willing to take drastic steps to insure that.

He made a sharp turn on one of the side streets when he spied a public phone. Because there was no telephone book, he called Welmer's office and asked his secretary to get him a number. When she did, he dialed, gave his information succinctly, and replaced the receiver. Phase One of the Plan had begun.

Nothing penetrated his thoughts. Not traffic,

not pedestrians, not sirens, not horns. Incisively, he thought through the steps. Bedelia wouldn't get away again.

Up one street, across another, then up again. Finally he took his bearings and took a cross street that would lead him into the old, still-stately neighborhood of his home.

Bedelia! No longer a child but a woman, aware of herself and her power, able to deal with whatever came. It was a physical wrench to recall the young girl who'd looked to him so trustingly. Now she needed no one. She'd made her own way. There was no need to look to anyone else. But what about de Linde? She'd loved another man.

The Plan twisted and turned in his mind, and he started to run.

By the time he was a block from his house, Dolph was drenched in perspiration, annoyed, and cursing steadily under his breath. He didn't like Bedeila or himself at that moment, but he had a purpose. He'd been out of control, but no more. The reins were in his hands now.

Making a sudden right turn, he strode down a brick alleyway that led to the avenue his health club was located on. Since he didn't have his athletic bag with him, he bought new swimtrunks. Then he went to the standard-size pool and swam length after length, not stopping until he'd swum two miles.

Not bothering with any of the other sports equipment, he returned to the locker room, barely speaking to the couple of men there that he knew. Dressing quickly in his damp, rumpled clothing, he hurried home. If physical exercise wouldn't chase her sensual image from his mind, perhaps work would.

For a few hours he buried himself in a new script that Welmer had given him that morning. Another owned by Delia Cosmetics International. In a short time he'd have to return to the West Coast and start work on the first one, *Southwind*. The male role in it was great, one he'd coveted.

Now this one. The role seemed to have been written just for him. Turning it down would be asinine, especially since Bedelia had offered him script control and the option to direct if he wished, just as on *Southwind*.

He read the piece through from front to back three times, speed-reading some, then pausing to concentrate on a segment. And it only got better.

Bedelia was manipulating him again. The plan took on greater dimensions.

He turned when the phone rang and picked it up. "Yes, you can print that," he told the excited woman on the other end. "It's accurate. Goodbye." He stared at the receiver. What would Bedelia think? He'd soon know. It would be in tomorrow's papers.

Thinking of that, he glanced at his watch. He would have to hurry and change if he was going to pick up Bedelia at six.

At ten minutes before six he was pacing the marble lobby of the building that housed Delia Cosmetics International. The building was new, a glass-and-steel marvel that soared into the sky. Did she lease her three floors, or was the whole place part of her holdings? How had she built up an international company in little more than ten years? Or had de Linde built it for her?

At six on the dot, the elevator doors opened, and Bedelia stepped out, greeting the security man on duty by name.

Dolph moved forward, thinking he'd never seen a more beautiful woman, ever. She could model her own products. Just looking at her was one of the most erotic experiences of his life. She was fresh, untouched; sophisticated, cosmopolitan; vulnerable, gamine. . . . Damn! How could she be such a mix of things? A wildly innocent woman of the world! And she'd dangled him on a string for years.

One thing he was very sure of at that moment. All his feelings about Bedelia, which he'd thought were dead and buried, had only been dormant, lying just beneath the surface. And like an inexorable force they were pushing themselves into his consciousness again, like a glacier on the move.

Obviously she kept a wardrobe at work. She'd changed from her business clothes to evening apparel. Her calf-length dress was made of tissue lamé, the fine weaving making it iridescent. No bead or bangle added unnecessary glitter. It swathed around her like another skin, its pale aqua hue making her eyes glint like freshly mined turquoise.

Her only accessory was one long filigreed earring that touched her bare shoulder, the quivering filaments catching every touch of light. Her long auburn hair was coiled atop her head in a knot. Her high-heeled shoes and clutch bag were of a muted turquoise hue, matching the dress.

"Hello," he said, stopping in front of her.

His voice ran up and down Bedelia's spine, prickling her skin. Resisting his magic, fighting that nebulous menace, her response was cooler than she intended. "Hello. Shall we go?"

He took her arm. "Are you very hungry?"

"Had you something in mind?"

The continental phrasing was like a fingernail on a blackboard to him. "Would that upset you?"

"Of course not."

"I thought we might go out and do something, work up an appetite so to speak."

Bedelia looked him over, stunned at how magnificent he looked in a midnight-blue silk suit, then gazed down at her dress. She needed a few seconds to get hold of herself. She'd never felt unsure when she'd been with Dolph back in Nice. Since meeting him again, she'd felt off-balance, her self-confidence shaken, and she didn't like that. She'd become used to being in control of her life, her destiny. Dolph had undermined a good share of that in a short time. There was something hidden. . . .

"Pardon me," she said, realizing he had spoken. "You said something."

"I was wondering why you were studying your dress and frowning. You look lovely." She looked so delectable, he wanted to take her back upstairs and make love to her in her executive office.

His silken voice made her shiver again. "Ah . . . you mentioned working up an appetite. Are we dressed for a run in the park?"

She dropped her gaze again. Looking at the floor was more comfortable than looking at Dolph.

He made her weak in the knees. Just like a silly groupie, she thought. Dolph Wakefield was consummately sexy . . . and dangerous.

"Dressed for it? Maybe. Armed for it? No." He took her arm and led her across the lobby. "We are dressed for dancing."

"Dancing?" Bedelia knew her mouth was open. She closed it. Still, she couldn't tear her gaze away from his lips. Too much sexuality. Her throat was a desert. Her blood beat a slow tattoo through her veins. Finally looking away from him, she glanced through the glass door. A meter maid was checking the license plate of a red Alfa Romeo Spider. "Is that your car being ticketed?"

"Damn! Hurry, Bedelia." He took her hand and squeezed her in with him in the quarter-opening of the revolving door. Keep her there! his libido cried. Ride around and around in the door, pressed tight to her.

"Hey!" Bedelia called to the meter maid, then hawled in a great gulp of air to steady herself. She hadn't been that close to Dolph in so long. It was downright shattering.

The meter maid looked up, her pen poised, a resigned, expectant look on her face. "No parking in the yellow zone," she said, cracking her gum.

"Be out of here in a second," Dolph said, and smiled at her.

Bedelia saw the woman's face change, her jaw drop, her eyes widen, the pen slip from nerveless fingers. Dolph Wakefield was still knocking them dead. She tried to smile, but there was vinegar in her mouth.

"You-you-you . . . Dolph Wakefield!" the woman

stuttered. "Gosh, I didn't know you were in town. Wait'll I tell my sister. She'll just die."

Dolph handed Bedelia into the car, then picked up the meter maid's pen. He handed it to her. "I know this isn't an easy job."

"Would you sign my ticket book?"

"Ah, where?"

"Right here, next to my name, please."

He looked up when he heard honking. He and the woman were blocking a lane of traffic, and he gestured toward the sidewalk.

The meter maid ignored that and glared at the man who'd honked. "Keep moving!" she bellowed. Then she looked back at Dolph and smiled widely. "Go ahead and sign. We're all right."

Dolph nodded, sliding a look at the angry driver trying to squeeze around them, then scribbled rapidly. "There you are. Thanks for your forbearance."

"You're welcome. Thanks for the autograph." She smiled. "And here's your ticket."

Dolph stared at the ticket, then at the woman sauntering down the avenue. When the horns started again, he slammed into the car.

Bedelia was doubled over, laughing.

"Very funny," he muttered, glancing at her. His heart turned over at the very real amusement pouring out of her, at her sparkling eyes, at the wonderful memories her laughter conjured. He and Bedelia had laughed so much when they'd been together. Seeing those even white teeth, her pink tongue protruding slightly between them, was a most erotic stimulus.

He forced sudden fantasies aside and started

the car. "Why didn't you stay out there and fight for me?" Engaging the gears, he moved smoothly into a break in traffic.

"Me? Interfere with that slick way you handled getting a ticket? Never." She wiped her eyes. "You thought she'd forget about the ticket."

He shifted against the seat belt, his smile rueful. "Yes, I did."

Bedelia laughed again. When was the last time she'd felt such delicious amusement! That summer in Nice?

"No need to hoot with laughter," Dolph told her tartly, even as he delighted in her gasps and giggles.

"How could I not? There are just not that many priceless moments in this world. And that one's in the top ten of all time. Dolph Wakefield getting his comeuppance!"

"You're a witch, Bedelia." He laughed with her.

For a second it was as though there hadn't been more than ten years and a million changes between them. Time telescoped to that moment and tied them in a golden knot. Laughter bound them and pulled them closer.

Neither breathed, as if afraid the slightest puff could blow away the precious sharing.

Then, mentally shaking herself, Bedelia smiled tremulously. The flash in time had evaporated.

Laughing with Dolph had sent her spinning back into the past. She hadn't had so much fun in ages. Yet there was a poignancy to it that made her eyes moisten. She strove for a light tone. "Poor baby. Your ego must be quivering with outrage."

Dolph took her hand in his. He needed to touch her, to feel her warmth. "And no one could enjoy that more than you."

Bedelia trembled with the joy of being free, with Dolph. His touch heated her through. How had she lived without it? Had she been a fool to put their togetherness on hold for so long? Uncertainty shook her. "It's just that you read the meter maid so wrong. She was bowled over by you, but nothing got in the way of the job. I'll bet she's the sole support of a family."

"Whatever, she outsmarted me." Dolph lifted her hand to his mouth and kissed her palm. "I thought only you could do that." When she stiffened and tried to free herself, his grip tightened.

"You have to shift," she said, her voice barely audible. She was coming apart. Her skin where his lips had clung burned and froze.

"I'll manage. Do you mind that I'm holding your hand?"

"Yes . . . No, of course not. But I'm safety-minded and—"

"I'll be careful." He couldn't release her. She warmed him, melted the iceberg of his soul. Yet he wasn't completely thawed. There was always the possibility she'd try to leave him again.

Resigned to having him hold her hand, she cast about for something to say. "You've been very successful over the years. Do you still like acting as much as you did?"

"Yes. Tell me about you. How did you get into cosmetics?"

"I mentioned my partner to you, André de

Linde. He was a chemist I met when I was studying at the Sorbonne. For years he'd made allergy-free creams for his wife, using vegetables and grains. After her death, he continued with his research. Then, when we met, he interested me in his work."

Dolph heard the sadness in her voice. His insides twisted. "You said he was a fine man."

"He was. He died just when we were starting our climb." She sighed, then noticed how rigid he'd become. Why? "Ah, I saw your picture with the race-car driver, Bear Kenmore, after he drove the Grand Prix in Europe."

"He won it too." Dolph grinned, shaking away the image of Bedelia with another man. "I want you to meet Bear and his wife and children. They have two boys. And I've another close friend, Piers Larraby. He and his wife have a boy and a girl."

"I don't remember you mentioning them when we lived in Nice."

Nice! Why had she said it that way? They'd lived *together!*

"I didn't know them then. I met Bear through Piers. They're old friends. Went to Harvard together. Piers I met late one night outside a bistro in Paris." He slanted a glance at her. "I was looking for you."

"Oh."

"Did you live with de Linde?" The words were out before he could stop them. "Sorry. That was none of my business."

"André was my mentor, my friend, and my partner. And when he died, he was seventy-eight years old."

Relief thundered through him. "I shouldn't have asked."

"No, you shouldn't. I don't need to ask about you. You and your women are plastered all over the trades."

"There weren't that many," Dolph shot back, stung at her remark. "And if I'd had half as much information about you as you had about me, I wouldn't need to ask any questions."

"I think you've fired that arrow already." She stared out the windshield, her hands shaking.

"If I have, it bears repeating."

"Really?" Her jaw was clenched so tight, her teeth ached. "If you're such a purist on communication, how is it you never returned my call? When you filmed *Retreat* in Paris, I called you and left a message."

"No!"

"Yes. And you never answered it."

"I never got it." She *had* called him. He believed her now. "That was seven years ago," he whispered.

"Yes."

Dolph sighted their destination with regret. The intimacy of being alone with Bedelia again, inhaling her essence, listening to her breathe, was potent. "Here we are." He pulled into the small semicircular drive in front of a club.

Bedelia looked at the facade, frowning. "Isn't this The Pillory? We can't go in there. It's private."

"As a descendant of Tory sympathizers during the Revolution, I can." Dolph was out of the car and around to her side before the attendant got there.

She looked up at him as he helped her out. "You're joking."

He grinned. "No. I had family on both sides of that war. Some remained here. Others returned to England."

"How like you to cover your bases," she said, not able to mask an answering grin.

As she preceded him into the club, he murmured in her ear, "That's one way a man gets what he wants, Bedelia."

She hesitated, a frisson of wariness rippling through her. "You sound resentful. Won't food turn to acid in your stomach?"

"I'll risk it."

She lifted her chin high. "As I recall, you had a mouth like a rapier when you were in a tantrum."

"Tantrum?" His mouth brushed her ear. "Why, darling, I'm in a full-blown fury with you." When she turned sharply, he kissed her on the mouth. "I think the maitre d' is waiting."

"I don't intend to dine with anyone who will try to bait me." She eyed him unblinkingly.

"Now who's angry? Don't deny it, Bedelia. I remember how your head went to one side whenever you were having a snit."

"Snit? Me!"

He urged her forward. His grip tightened on her arm when he felt the infinitesimal arching of her body, as though she would pull away from him. "Good evening, Nelson," he greeted the maitre d'. "Is the orchestra in good tune this evening?"

The maitre d' allowed his mouth to stretch in a small smile. "As always, our music pleases, Mr.

Wakefield. It's good to see you, sir. You have come to dance? Perhaps to dine?"

"Dancing, I think, Nelson. And some of your hot canapes. We'll decide on dinner later."

Nelson didn't snap-salute. It just seemed that way. Then he led them along a passage lined with greenery, the low murmurs of diners and clinks of cutlery barely penetrating the curtain.

The room he led them to made Bedelia gasp.

Two-stories high, with a balcony on the upper level for people to look down upon the dancers, the room was swathed in champagne-hued sheers. They matched the walls and the drapes over the tall arched windows. Even the crystal chandeliers were touched with gold. It was a slice of yesteryear London.

Bedelia smiled.

"You like it," Dolph said. "I'm glad." That her happiness could give him such pleasure jolted him—and set the Plan in concrete.

"I like it very much. And it has a fine reputation." She smiled at the maitre d', ignoring Dolph who held her chair. Had he kissed her neck? No. It must have been a draft.

"Canape board and champagne," Dolph ordered.

"And may I have Saratoga Water?" Bedelia added.

Nelson nodded and moved away.

"You drank wine in Nice," Dolph said.

"I wasn't as smart as I am now."

"Does that mean that if I drink the champagne, I'm not too intelligent?"

"It'll mean you prefer champagne to Saratoga Water. I don't." She glanced at him and wished she hadn't. Merely looking at him made her want to jump over the table and into his lap. She tried to look away, but his gaze had captured hers. She had to say something before she *did* something foolish.

"Didn't you say we were going to dance?" Oh, Lord! Did she have to say *that*? Being held by Dolph could destroy her last defenses. She was definitely making some wrong moves.

"I did."

Dolph rose to his feet and held his hand out to her. He noticed her slight hesitation before she put her hand in his, noticed the trembling in her hand. Good, he thought. She hadn't become *too* sophisticated.

Following her out to the dance floor was a pleasure. Her tall lissome body swayed gently, and her small hips and well-rounded backside were the most enticing picture he'd ever encountered.

He took her into his arms, and memories flooded through him. Pressing his lips to her hair, he swung her close to his body. "Remember the night we danced on the beach?"

They'd been naked! she thought, alarmed. "Vaguely." Her husky voice gave her away though.

"Then we watched the sunrise over the sea. It was beautiful."

They'd just made love! Their bodies moist with love dew, they'd held each other. Bedelia tried to tamp out the vision.

Their bodies swayed as one.

"For breakfast I said I wanted—"

"Dolph, I'm listening to the music."

But that didn't stop her memories. Dolph had

said he wanted her for breakfast. And she'd told him to feel free and take his fill!

An unseen hand seemed to nudge her closer to him. And she didn't mean to close her eyes. They shut by themselves. And then she was whirling with the music and the man into the world of delight that had once been theirs.

Five

They danced and danced, long past the dinner hour and into the night, lost in each other and their shared times. Caught in a web of memories neither could get free of, they nibbled on shrimp, crackers, and crab, fruit glazed with Camembert, hot slices of brie.

"I like cheese and fruit," Bedelia said dazedly.

"Good for you." Dolph popped a grape into his mouth, then sipped his champagne. "Would you like to dance again?" He wanted her back in his arms.

"Yes." It felt so good to hold him.

They rarely sat out a number. Conversation was sparse. Eye contact was fleeting.

"Good food." Had she eaten a grape between two crackers?

"Excellent." Though caviar had never been a favorite of his, he spread it on brie and ate the concoction.

"Do you think government bonds are a good investment?" she asked, wondering if it was possible to get lost in his eyes. Lord, he was beautiful.

"What government?" Her skin was wonderful, satiny. He wanted to kiss all of it.

"Right. That is a consideration." A faint shadow of beard accentuated the strong line of his jaw. How often she'd kissed him there.

His gaze fixed on the neckline of her dress. In his imagination his mouth followed that line as his hands—

"Dolph? Are you choking?"

"No, no, just swallowed the wrong way." His body had hardened. He wanted to remove that beautiful dress and . . . "Shall we dance?"

Bedelia blinked. "All right."

Pressing against his lean body was heaven. She had to resist the urge not to wriggle. His skin had always been so smooth. Was it still?

"Why did you sigh, Bedelia?" It had sounded like those damn little sounds she'd made when he was kissing her navel, or running his tongue up her bare back.

"Oh. Did I step on your foot? You groaned," she said.

"Knee problems." She felt so good in his arms, her lower body undulating against his.

"Should we sit down?"

"No!"

People turned to look at them.

"Good." Bedelia was glad when he held her close, tucking her head on his shoulder. It had been so long! And she'd missed him so much. More nights than she cared to remember, she had awakened bathed in perspiration because she'd dreamed that Dolph rejected her. Those nights she'd get up, throw cold water on her face, change her sheets, and curl into a miserable ball of loneliness.

"You really called me, Bedelia?"

She lifted her head and nodded. It had taken all of her strength to keep to the covenant she'd made to herself when she'd fled to Paris. One day she would stand on her own, be her own person. No one would interfere with her then. On that day, she promised herself, she would face Dolph and see if they could recapture what they had.

But why had she waited so long? She could have gone to him years ago. And had she truly needed to leave him in the first place?

When the band signed off, Dolph released her reluctantly.

"We've only had canapes," she said. "Would you like to share a casserole at my place? Lorette will have prepared something."

"I'd like that." He didn't want to part from her.

"Good." Maybe she should have listened to her French friends, she thought. Have an affair, they told her. It was only natural. Only wise. But trying to imagine herself with another man, loving him as she'd loved Dolph, had been impossible. Life without even the hope of being with Dolph again would be shades of gray.

As he drove them across town, they didn't speak, didn't look at each other. Bedelia felt shy when she unlocked the door to her place.

"You can freshen up in that room," she said as she led him to the second floor of the apartment.

"Thank you."

In her bedroom she stared at her reflection. He was there in her home, in the middle of the night. The only man she'd ever been intimate with, the only man who'd ever filled her life, was no longer a world away. He was mere steps away. And she was scared witless.

Was the magic gone? Was there any fire left? Had his tastes changed?

Bedelia's hand shook, slashing lipstick up from the corner of her mouth. "It's all right." The sound of her own voice jarred her. "No matter what happens, you'll keep going, Bedelia."

A wrenching grief pulled at her at the thought of losing Dolph forever.

Dolph looked around the bedroom, absently noting the richness. Bedelia lived here!

He used the bathroom, studying the color scheme, the accoutrements. When had he ever cared about interior decorating? He'd always told decorators his preferences and let them take it from there. Now he looked at everything, studied it all, wanting any information he could glean.

Back in the bedroom, he stared at the fabric wallpaper, feeling a little annoyed. He liked her home, liked the touches, could feel her in the rooms.

In his daydreams of Bedelia, and there'd been more than he cared to admit, he'd always pictured her returning to him, looking much the same as she always had. Flinging her arms around him, she'd hold him tightly, telling him she'd never let him go.

Nothing had thrown him more than when he'd seen her for the first time that day. What could he offer her now that a thousand men couldn't match?

He took a deep breath. Holding her in his arms again had brought back so many memories, so many torrid, sweet, loving recollections. His body sang with the familiarity of touching her. His desire for her hadn't abated. He hoped the evening had had the same effect on her.

Inhaling deeply, he crossed the room and opened the door.

He saw her at once as she came out of a room on the opposite side of the bridge overlooking the foyer. He stayed still, studying her. She hadn't really lost that sweet touch of innocence. She still retained that vulnerability, that sense of wonder that had been part of her when she was nineteen. It hadn't all disappeared. But now the patina of success and maturity had ripened her beauty, fulfilling the promise that had been there when she was younger. Damn! She was downright gorgeous, and though she was obviously aware of herself as a woman and a businessperson, all of her outer sheen couldn't quite mask a touch of breathless youth.

"Hello," he said quietly.

Startled, Bedelia looked up, her lips parted. "Hello yourself." Her heart rose in her throat at the sight of him. Were there strands of gray in his sun-streaked blond hair? He had wonderful skin, clear and unblemished . . . all over.

She turned away from him, feeling hot. Her imagination was too unruly.

"I like your place," he said. Not that he could look at anything but her. She'd only freshened her makeup, yet she looked even more beautiful than she had a few minutes ago. What power she had!

Did he like it enough to live in it? she wondered, and bit her lip. She'd almost said it, almost asked. He could topple her world for her, cut her down to what she'd been before she'd built herself. It had taken so much strength to buttress herself against her stepbrother, to become independent enough to meet Dolph on equal terms. But did she have enough strength now? Stricken, she stared at him.

"What is it?" he asked softly. He saw her expression change, here eyebrows draw together, her features tighten, as though she'd pulled in on herself. "Tell me. Is it a headache?" He moved toward her swiftly, his arms outstretched. Not all the protestations from his common sense, telling him she had too much of him already, kept him from cuddling her close to him.

Reeling with the shock of the feelings that swamped her, Bedelia clung to him, letting her head lie on his chest in the old remembered way. "Just a little headache," she said. "I guess I need food." Not to mention other things. Having him hold her, touch her, kiss her. Damn her mind. It wouldn't shut down. And she wasn't remotely hungry. She was sure she'd eaten a ton of canapes at The Pillory.

Dolph kept his arm around her and led her to the stairs. "I'll make you something."

"I'm sure there's food in the refrigerator, waiting to be put in the microwave. Lorette will be sleeping. I can't break her of the habit of rising at five." She smiled shakily.

He touched her nose with one finger. "Maybe that's because I'm not living here with you. She's old-fashioned and believes the man—"

"No, sir, she doesn't buy into any of that macho stuff," Bedelia said spiritedly. "Remember how she handled the greengrocer in Nice? She's a modern woman who believes men and women are equal."

Dolph laughed. "Does she, now? Well, that shouldn't be a problem. I agree with her." He gazed down at Bedelia again. Her skin was luscious, opalescent, soft but firm. He wanted to kiss every inch of it. His heart pounded heavily at the thought. "Come on, let's see what we can find. Food will take care of your headache."

In the kitchen he gestured to the high-backed stools on one side of the working island. His gaze flitted over the various cooking pans of copper and steel that hung above their heads. Opposite the island was a French ceramic stove that would have cost thousands of dollars to import. Lorette had a cook's heaven. "This is how you blackmailed her?" he asked. "With costly kitchen equipment?"

Bedelia lifted her chin. "Blackmail? Ridiculous. She wanted to come to America." She recalled his sardonic look from their time in Nice. When his lashes all but covered his eyes, his mouth would take that lovable upward twist, making her breath catch in her throat.

"Do you have a medicine chest down here?" At her puzzled look, he added, "Aspirin. Remember?"

"What? Oh, yes—that. There's aspirin in the pantry on the second shelf from the top, along with other medications."

Maybe it wasn't a good idea to have him there, she thought. He was chipping away at her defenses with those eyes, that smile. . . .

Dolph could see she was uncomfortable. That didn't displease him. She'd been orchestrating things for too long. He ambled into the pantry, finding what he wanted at once.

Filling a glass with cold water, he handed her two tablets.

"I'll just take one," she said, feeling like a fraud as she swallowed.

"Now, sit there, and I'll get something for us." He shook his head, his grin rueful. "It's my fault. I should have fed you before taking you dancing."

"No, no, it's nothing. Really. It's fading. I had so many canapes."

He leaned down and kissed her cheek, his mouth lingering there. "Relax. I won't poison you."

"No? How do I know that? Lorette did all the cooking in Nice." Why did she mention that?

Once more, memories crowded them. They couldn't look away from each other. Swimming naked in the sea. Rolling on the bed in the throes of laughter and passion.

"So she did," he said after a minute. "I've picked up a few pointers since then." He pushed back from her with an effort. Homing in on the refrigerator, he blindly opened the door and took out the first thing at hand.

"Yes, that must be what she fixed for me," Bedelia said, glancing at the casserole dish. She slipped off the stool and moved toward the microwave. "What is it?"

"What? Oh. Ah, a cassoulet. Lamb, I think." He took the written instructions off the top. When she opened the door of the microwave, he set the dish inside, then watched Bedelia punch in the required numbers.

"So how's your stepbrother these days?" He hoped Orton was in traction from toe to eyebrow.

Bedelia's laugh was tight. "About the same. Still wanting money for harebrained schemes. He drops by the office every few weeks. Lydia wants to throw him out her window."

"Hooray for Lydia."

Dolph smiled, but she could see his lingering anger. Orton better not try to approach him again, she thought, and she would tell her stepbrother that the next time she saw him.

Together, she and Dolph hunted up utensils and napkins. In minutes they were seated across from each other at the island, politely passing the cassoulet and doling out salad to each other.

They automatically ate the delicately flavored, herb-scented dish, not speaking. Bedelia couldn't figure out why Dolph had suddenly become so constrained, and didn't know what to say to him. But perhaps some distance between them was a good thing."

"I enjoyed seeing you," he said as she walked him to the door.

"It was fun." Great, she thought. She sounded like a disenchanted teenager.

He smiled, kissed her cheek, and left.

After locking the door behind him, she climbed the stairs, talking to herself. "Damn, I should have sat closer to him. No. He exudes too much atomic energy. I acted like an adolescent."

That night she dreamed of Dolph, dreamed he laughed at her when she told him she still loved him.

Dolph paced the floor most of the night, wondering what Bedelia would say about the Plan. She'd have some idea about it in the morning. He wanted her. His being ached for her. Yet he couldn't tamp down his fury when he thought of how for all those years she'd known about him and he'd been totally in the dark about her. Well, she'd have an inkling about how he felt in the morning. The Plan was in operation.

Bedelia rose from her bed and stumbled to the bathroom. A bona fide headache was somewhat assuaged by her shower and shampoo. Dressing in a green Chanel suit, she donned deep brown and cream leather pumps, then picked up her brown briefcase.

"Sliced peaches, Mademoiselle Deel-y-a," Lorette announced when Bedelia entered the kitchen. "I got them from the market this morning. And fresh orange juice. Here is the paper too. Your picture is very good. So is the M'sieur's."

"Oh?" Bedelia murmured distractedly as she sat down in the sunny room off the kitchen. Then she shot a sharp look at the beatifically smiling housekeeper. "Mine? Dolph's?" Bedelia had sipped a good portion of her juice and eaten half of her oat bran with peaches before she opened the paper to the right page.

"Aagh!"

When Bedelia surged to her feet, making growling sounds, Lorette tried to calm her. "Are you ill, mademoiselle? Did you want your breakfast in bed?"

"Ill? I'm sick with anger. I'm furious. I'm fighting mad. I'll sue. I'll kill him." Bedelia hauled in deep shuddering breaths, waving the paper in the air.

Baffled, her reading ability in English limited, Lorette stared at the paper, then at Bedelia. "You don't like the picture."

"I'll dismember him." Bedelia threw down the paper and stalked to the telephone. Before she could pick it up, it rang.

"Bedelia Fronsby," she answered.

"Is it true you'll be living in Europe now, Miss—"

She slammed down the phone. "Get this number changed, Lorette. This morning."

"You should have had your breakfast in bed," Lorette pronounced sagely. She squinted at the almost empty dish of oat bran. "Too much roughage, *hein?*"

"Absolutely not." Bedelia picked up the phone again and dialed into her computer information. She wrote down the number it gave her, then dialed again, carrying the phone back to the table. Drumming her fingers, she waited through three rings. When she heard Dolph's recorded voice announcing that he couldn't come to the phone right now, she slammed down the receiver.

"How dare he," she muttered to Lorette, "put an announcement in the paper that we're getting married!"

Lorette shrugged. "You should be glad. You love him." She gave her employer a superior smile and sailed into the kitchen.

"I do not!" Bedelia shouted to the still swinging door. "He has no integrity, and he's a womanizer."

Lorette's head popped through the door again. "That will not happen when you marry him," she said seriously. "M'sieur will be a good husband. Just you keep him in bed for a while. Then he will forget all the beautiful women and think only of you." She disappeared once more.

Bedelia was sputtering. "You're fired. Go back to France," she said when she got her breath.

Lorette's head appeared again. "You'll be late. And throw cold water on your face. It's red."

"Traitor."

"Tch, tch. Do not grind your teeth, mademoiselle, or you will lose them. You are not as young as you used to be."

Bedelia glared at the swinging door, then gathered up her purse and briefcase and slammed out of the apartment. In the downstairs lobby, she shoved the outside door open, intent on catching a cab. She stopped, though, when she saw a herd of reporters outside the building, bullying the immutable doorman.

Retreating back into the lobby, she used the phone to call for a taxi to pick her up on the cross street at the back of her building.

Since rush hour was at its height, the cab didn't arrive for more than fifteen minutes. The short drive to her office passed quickly, though. Because she expected more reporters at the office, she told the driver to leave her at the rear entrance. Using her key, she went in the delivery door and took a back elevator up.

Lydia was frazzled and a little touchy. "It's been insane round here. Security kept its night shift on to help the day people hold off the reporters and local groupies."

"Hold all my calls. And get Mr. Wakefield on the line."

"He's in your office," Lydia said stiffly.

"What?" Bedelia threw open the door. He was lounging in her chair as if he belonged there! She slammed the door and stalked to the desk. Her hands curled into fists, she leaned across the desk, looking him straight in the eye. "Explain!"

"Lower your voice, darling. Lydia will think we're fighting." Immense satisfaction flooded over him as he contemplated her red face and angry tone.

"We are," she said in a slightly softer voice.

"You look wonderful when you're angry. Like a sexy Valkyrie."

"And I'll haul you off to Valhalla if you don't tell me what's going on, Dolph Wakefield."

"My, my, you are in a temper."

Her whole body shivered with awareness at his

silky tone. Why in hell was *he* angry? "Aren't you the one who submitted the story?"

"You know me so well, love." The tone didn't change.

"They even put in the wedding date. Two weeks from today," Bedelia said tightly, stepping back from the desk to stand erect. "What's going on?"

"I put the story in. We are getting married and—" He glared at her phone as the intercom buzzer sounded, then snatched up the receiver.

Poleaxed, Bedelia did nothing but stare as he spoke to her secretary.

"All right," he said, "send them in. I've been expecting them."

"Who?" Bedelia's voice was little more than a croak. Dolph rose to his feet and strode around the desk. His arm around her waist, he turned her to face the door.

"Who—?"

"Shh, you sound like an owl," he said sweetly.

Bedelia trembled with pent-up temper, pushing hard at his arm to get free.

The door opened, and two men walked in, grinning. They were handsome and vaguely familiar. "Who—?"

"Bedelia loves to ask questions," Dolph said, interrupting her. He shook hands with the men. "How are you, Piers? Bear?"

The two men nodded perfunctorily, their gazes on Bedelia.

Bedelia felt as though she were being inspected. Her chin lifted. "Who are you? And what are you doing in my office?"

"Darling, these are my best friends, though I

hadn't met them when we were together in Nice. Piers Larraby. Bear Kenmore. Bedelia Fronsby."

Piers took her hand, smiling. "I'm glad you're back. Dolph's waited a long time." His grin widened when her mouth dropped open.

"Has he?" she asked faintly.

Bear pushed his friend aside and caught Bedelia up in his arms. "Yes, he has, but I can see why he waited." He glanced at Dolph. "Bedelia, do you think you can keep him from killing me? He doesn't like me holding you." He lowered her to her feet gently.

"That's just tough," she said, finding her voice and some of her balance. "Everything isn't going to go his way. No matter what he thinks."

Piers laughed. "Atta girl. You sound like my lady. Which reminds me, I'm to invite both of you to dinner at Bear's place. We have to celebrate the coming nuptials. Bear's family will be there, and we've promised the children they can stay up for a short time, so you'll have to come early."

"And, Dolph," Bear said, "Mother and Dad will probably insist that the reception be held at their place."

"It's all taken care of," Dolph said. "The Pillory is handling everything."

"Everything?" Bedelia enunciated every syllable. Tense silence sizzled through the room.

Piers and Bear looked at the newly affianced pair, then gazed at each other. They smiled.

"Ah, well, I'm glad you called," Bear said to Dolph. "It would've killed Kip to read that in the newspaper."

"That's how I found out," she muttered. Then

her back arched when Dolph tightly gripped her around the waist.

"What?" Piers's smile widened as Dolph grimaced. "You disconcerted, Dolph? I love it."

"Very funny," Dolph said acerbically.

"I think so," Bear said.

"It's nothing," Dolph said. "There are just a few loose ends that haven't been seen to yet, but we'll handle it."

"I'll bet." Piers laughed. When Dolph's eyes narrowed, his mirth increased. "I know, I know. Whatever it is you've cooked up, you don't want us in on it."

"That's the feeling I got," Bear said, smiling.

Piers snapped his fingers. "Damn, I'd love to hang around for this, but I guess we'd better go, Bear." He leaned down and kissed Bedelia's cheek.

"Yeah." Bear did the same. "I'd take down that wonderful painting if you decide to start something. Unless my eyes are going, that's a Wyeth."

"It's a Wyeth," Bedelia said flatly. She didn't look at the two friends as they backed toward the door. Her gaze was fixed on Dolph Wakefield.

"Wish we could stay longer," Piers said. "It brings back sweet memories just thinking about it. Boy, Damiene and I used to have some rare spats."

"Piers, I think Dolph is getting steamed," Bear said softly. "Let's go."

"Right. So long. It was nice meeting you, Bedelia."

"It was nice meeting both of you," she said, trying to smile.

"So long," Bear said, and pushed Piers out the door.

Neither Dolph nor Bedelia noticed when the door closed.

"Now, relax, Bedelia—"

"You called your friends, but you didn't think you needed to call me, warn me, *ask* me!"

He shrugged, watching her right hand inch toward an ornate Florentine inkstand. "Remember what Bear said about the Wyeth."

"I should paste you with this," she said, feeling light-headed with anger. "We are not getting married."

"We are," he said quietly.

She blinked at the sudden menace she saw in his eyes. "You're angry. I'm the one who has been worked over by your scam—"

"You? Worked over? What do you call more than a decade without a call, without a line or a sign of recognition? What did you expect? Roses? Accolades? Applause?" His voice rose a few decibels with each query.

"I told you I called. And left a message."

"*Once.* In all those years you tried to call me *once.*"

"Don't raise your voice to me, Dolph Wakefield."

"I damn well should do more than that." His voice went up another notch.

"Oh, you should, should you? You pull a stunt like this and *you* get angry?"

Her own fury rose with his. Some still rational part of her wondered when he had developed such a temper. She'd rarely seen that side of him. Only when Orton had intruded on their idyll had she seen his anger. In fact, if she'd been asked any time before that day if Dolph Wakefield had a temper, she would have resoundingly said no. Control. That was the word that described Dolph. And dedicated to his work. But edgy, snappy, testy? Up until now, no.

"And don't try to put me off by acting injured about the past," she charged on. But her next salvo died when she saw his color change from red to chalky white.

"Acting?" he repeated in a soft, deadly voice. "There's no acting involved. What you did damn near killed me, Bedelia Fronsby!"

"I—I didn't mean it quite that way. And I never expected anything from you. If—"

He swiped at the air, cutting her off. "Wrong. You expected a lot from me. You expected to oversee me, watch me for endless years, then come out of the woodwork. You pinned me like a butterfly in a collection. Well, you're not calling all the shots, sweetheart."

"Woodwork? Me? I did not come out of the woodwork. I have spent more than ten years building an international business and—"

"I know the stats. And I'm telling you that you don't control our lives anymore. From now on I have a say—"

"Now wait a minute—"

"No, you wait. I've talked to my lawyer, a staff of them actually. I have that tape we made together, where you promise to come and stay with me—"

"You've still got that?" Oh, Lord, she thought. Another painful memory. She could recall that night so vividly, the two of them giggling over a bottle of champagne, reading love poetry to each other, and exchanging vows while they recorded their own silliness.

Taking a deep breath, she rallied herself. "What difference does that make? It's not admissible—"

"Don't give me legalese, lady. You're not a lawyer. And mine say it constitutes a convenant of a kind, and a case can be made for breach of promise. I told them to search out anything that gives me a hold over you."

"You wouldn't dare." Her voice was a mere whisper.

He leaned closer to her. "Wouldn't I? You'd be a fool to believe that. Because I'll use it, Bedelia. You either marry me, or I'm going to sue the pants off you and your damned corporation. Got that?"

Anger built like a fierce windstorm. Bedelia was burning hot, ready to do mayhem. Not since she'd started her climb had she'd felt so out of control. "You can't do that!"

"Watch me. Which is it, Bedelia? Marrying me at St. Francis of Assisi Mission here in New York? Or going to court here and in London?"

"London?" Her voice had a squeak to it.

"Maybe even Paris. I intend to take this to every court I can."

"My lawyers will have something to say about this," she managed to say in a stronger voice.

He shrugged. "No doubt. But my people are competent, and they're building a case." He strode to her and pulled her into his arms before she could move back.

Kissing her was one of the things that had

plagued his memory over the years. It couldn't be as good as his recollections had painted it. No, he thought as he lowered his mouth to hers. It wasn't like his memories. It was much, much more. Better, wonderful, warm, exciting. He felt her resistance, and it only fired his determination.

His mouth opened on hers, taking, giving.

Bedelia fought the heat, the overwhelming passion. Frozen Idol, the gossip columnists called him. Not now, not here. Yet with the heat, she could feel hard ice deep down. Still, her senses whirled as desire spread through her, pouring from him into her in unending streams. It was like Nice . . . but different, deeper, more poignant and more wonderful. She shivered.

He lifted his head reluctantly. "Chilled, darling? Don't worry. After we're married, I intend to see that you're never cold again. I'll be back to pick you up at six." He kissed her quickly, then spun on his heel and left.

Bedelia swayed, staring at the closed door, her hand pressed to her mouth. Though heated blood thundered through her, she felt bereft and cold without him.

Bedelia dressed for the evening in her office again. She took little notice of the rust-colored satin suit, with its figure-hugging jacket and very straight skirt with two kick pleats on one side. The twisted gold buttons matched her gold earrings and the pin fastened to her lapel. Her cream satin blouse had a ruffled front, and long ruffled cuffs hung below the sleeves of the jacket. Her shoes and clutch bag were of rust-colored kid.

Brushing her hair out of the tight chignon she wore for work, she let it sweep around her shoulders. Staring blindly at her reflection in the powder room mirror, she wondered why she hadn't just told Dolph she wouldn't go with him.

She didn't notice the door swing open.

"Hello," Dolph said from behind her. "Lydia told me you were dressing. You look beautiful."

The powder room was spacious, including a small closet and dressing table, but with Dolph in it, it took on Lilliputian proportions. Bedelia pressed back against the dressing table. "Hello. I thought I locked that door."

"You didn't. Shall we go?"

He looked gorgeous in a dark evening suit. "You're very formal."

"I dress up for you, Bedelia. A change from when we wore nothing in Nice."

It took all her strength to swallow the gasp. She swept around him and into her office. "I'm ready."

"So am I. What do you suggest?"

"Dinner," she said bitingly.

"Aw, I thought surely you wanted to—"

"Your car or mine?"

He smiled. "Mine is downstairs."

How could she have ever loved that smile?

Bedelia didn't look at him as they rode down in the elevator. She could feel his gaze on her though.

Dolph leaned against the wall, staring at her, wanting her. He ached with desire. All his preconceived notions of how he would handle their first meetings hadn't included that. Bedelia still drew him as no other woman ever had. Maybe he had wanted to jab at her when he put the notice of their marriage in the paper, but he hadn't counted on the unmitigated joy it gave him to contemplate being her husband.

He pulled her hand through his arm as they walked through the lobby. "Safety," he explained.

"A security force patrols this building," she said tartly.

"Good." He didn't release her until he handed her into his illegally parked car.

He hadn't gotten another ticket. That irked Bedelia. Where were the meter maids when you needed them?

The Manhattan evening was magical. The air was mild, and against her will she relaxed against the soft leather seat. When Dolph reached out to her, her fingers curled around his as though they had a life of their own.

"Bear has a place here in town," he said. "Piers's home is out on the island."

Bedelia could hear the warmth in his voice. "They mean a great deal to you."

He nodded abruptly. "Sometimes I think they saved my sanity."

She didn't want to pursue that, and was glad that less than a minute later, he pulled over to the curb and parked.

Dolph helped her from the car, drawing her arm through his again. She looked up at the four-story brownstone, set in the middle of a quiet block on the upper East Side. "It's a beautiful place."

Dolph nodded, leading her to the door. It opened before he could press the bell. "Bear."

"I was watching for you. Come in, Bedelia, and meet the gang."

Bedelia entered the high wide foyer. Instantly a door at the other end banged open, and two boys, as alike as peas in a pod, scampered toward them.

"Simmer down," Bear said mildly, reaching for them.

They evaded him and cannoned right into Bedelia, who would have fallen if Dolph hadn't caught her.

"Hi, guys," he said. "This is my lady, not yours." Although she'd regained her balance, he kept his arms around her.

Bedelia would have argued that point with him if she hadn't been so entranced with the giggling twins. She had little experience with children, but she guessed they were about three years old. "Hi. I'm Bedelia."

"I'm Pat-rick Dol-thus," one said, "and he's Piers Dol-thus." Patrick pointed to Dolph, grinning. "He's our godfather."

Bedelia bent down so she was their height. "It's nice to meet you."

Piers Adolphus smiled shyly.

Patrick Adolphus grinned. "We know who you are. We heard Daddy tell Mommy that you'll have pretty babies 'cuz—"

"Good Lord." Bear scooped the twins into his arms and smiled sheepishly at Bedelia. "I try never to talk when they're around, but sometimes I slip up. Stop laughing, Dolph. Bedelia's embarrassed."

"No, she's not, are you, darling?"

"Ah, no." She wanted to sink through the floor. She didn't look at Dolph, still chuckling as they followed Bear into a spacious room. Oriental rugs and French cloth wallpaper were a beautiful background for the stunning women who faced her.

Piers stepped forward to take her hand and lead her to the woman.

"I'm Kip Kenmore," the leggy golden blond woman said. She grimaced. "And I heard the town crier."

Bedelia thought that Kip Kenmore was lovely, her wide-set eyes sensuous and appealing.

"Mine aren't much better," the other woman said. "I'm Damiene Larraby."

"Hello. I'm Bedelia Fronsby." Bedelia wondered if this trim woman with stunning silver-blond hair, had ever modeled for *Vogue.*

"And these are mine," Damiene went on, gesturing to a girl and boy. "This is Tabitha, who's four, and this is Beryl Adolphus, who's just two."

"Godfather, again?" Bedelia asked. Dolph nodded proudly.

"But I don't talk like the boys," Tabitha said primly. "And I'm Uncle Dolph's favorite." When the adults chuckled, the child's smile widened.

"Should I tell her I have a new favorite?" Dolph whispered in Bedelia's ear.

She blushed and moved away, not answering.

As Bear got drinks for everyone and Damiene and Kip served hors d'oeuvres, Bedelia felt amazingly warm and comfortable. She laughed and joked with the others as though she'd known them for years.

After the children went to bed, they sat down to a delicious meal of Cornish hen. Although no one said anything, Bedelia knew Dolph's friends were curious about how she and Dolph had met again. Not wanting to reveal her own subterfuge, she decided she could at least tell them about his failure at charming the meter maid.

They loved it. Piers and Bear howled with laughter, and Kip had to wipe away tears.

"Oh, Dolph," she said. "I wish I could have seen that."

"Me too," Damiene said, leaning close to his cheek.

"Traitors," Dolph said, but he smiled at the two women.

After they'd said good night and were driving back to her place, Bedelia looked at Dolph. "I can see why they're so important to you."

"They're my family and friends. Sometimes they were all the warmth I had these past years."

Coldness entered the car. Bedelia moved closer to the door. Dolph could have bitten his tongue.

Six

The next day Bedelia handled business, gave a pat explanation to any queries, and kept smiling. She and Dolph had parted stiffly the night before, but he'd reminded her forcefully that the engagement stood.

After a lunch meeting that had stretched her endurance to the limit, Bedelia longed to curl up on the cream-colored couch under the Wyeth painting and sleep for four years. She had half-risen, telling herself she'd lie down just for a minute, when her intercom buzzer rang. She picked up the receiver. "Yes, Lydia."

"It's your stepbrother. He insists on— Wait! You can't do that."

The door swung open.

Bedelia fixed a hard glare on Orton. "If you ever press the door opener on Lydia's desk again, I'll have you thrown out of here. Maybe even arrested. And you won't be allowed on the premises again. Clear?"

Orton hadn't changed much over the years. He had less hair and more of a paunch, and she saw now more noticeable signs of dissipation and self-indulgence. His skin was putty-hued, as though he never took a walk in the sun. He had always considered a good diet and exercise a waste of time. What would Dolph think of him after all this time?

"It's all right, Lydia," she said when her secretary appeared in the doorway behind Orton. "I'll handle it."

Orton glared at Lydia as she closed the door. "You should get better help."

"You should get out of here," Bedelia said. "I'm busy. We have nothing to say to each other." He still annoyed her more than anyone else she knew. No doubt he'd read the article Dolph had put in the paper and had come to taunt her.

"I think we have a lot to say," he told her. "I want a part of your corporation. Other times I've asked. Now I'm insisting. Oh, not all of it." He sat down in the chair in front of her desk, then lifted the Florentine inkstand, examining it. "Nice I like things like this. Mind if I keep it?"

"Yes, I mind. And no, you may not keep it. If you try to take anything from this office, I'll call the police." She smiled at him. "You know I mean it. Now get out of here. I've told you countless times that I've no intention of letting you into my company. I mean it."

Orton frowned and replaced the inkstand. "You haven't been listening. You were always too abrupt, Bedelia. I don't want a job. I want a partnership. And if I don't get it, I'm going to sell my story to the tabloids. All about my sister Lolita who lived with Dolph Wakefield years ago as his mistress."

Icy dread shivered up her spine. "That's old news, and nobody is interested." Dredging up all that misery would be a torture.

Orton rocked the chair onto its back two legs. "I doubt anyone connects Delia of Delia Cosmetics with Dolph Wakefield's pet whore of ten years ago. But I know the story, and I can prove it." He looked at his nails, then around her office. "I like this office. It would suit me."

The Florentine inkstand hit him in the chest. The chair toppled backward, tossing him end over teakettle. He landed on all fours, mouth agape, sputtering, shocked.

Bedelia might have laughed had she not been so burdened by frustration and outrage. Maybe if Dolph hadn't tackled her with his newspaper article, maybe if she hadn't felt so cornered, maybe if she didn't see all the control she'd fought for fading away, she wouldn't have done it. Maybe.

She whipped around the desk, picking up the inkstand and brandishing it like a weapon before Orton could right himself. "Now you get out of here. And don't ever come back. You'll not get one penny from me, cretin, and so you may tell every tabloid in the world."

The door burst open, and Lydia was there, a heavy metal mailing tube in her hand. "I heard the noise and thought there might be trouble. Did you coldcock him?"

"I don't know. Maybe. What does that mean?"

Bedelia didn't take her eyes off the sputtering Orton as he scrambled to his feet.

He shook his fist at her. "Damn you, Bedelia, you could have broken something. I'll sue."

"Sue away, Orton. You'll get nothing from me. I have some very able lawyers who would be glad to get you into court. This garbage is leaving, Lydia. Call Security and see that he's escorted from the building and never allowed to return."

"I called them when I heard the noise," Lydia said grimly, waving her mailing tube. "He won't come back."

"How dare you speak to me that way?" Orton shouted at Lydia. "You are a mere minion here, while I one day will be running this corporation. You'll rue the day you were uncivil."

"In a pig's eye," said the redoubtable Lydia, standing back as two stalwart security men arrived. "Throw him in the Dumpster."

The guards led Orton from the office.

Bedelia wanted to laugh. To cry. To scream. "No more callers, Lydia. I don't care if the King of England is on the phone."

"They have a queen over there, so don't fret yourself." Lydia closed the door.

Bedelia sat down at her desk and put her head in her hands. Maybe it was all a bad dream.

At six o'clock, Dolph strolled into her office, frowning. "Lydia made dark noises, as though you've had some trouble."

" 'Dark' being the operative word." Bedelia rose and strolled over to the floor-to-ceiling window.

To her jaundiced eyes the pinkish aura of the sky from the setting of the sun looked ominous. The world was topsy-turvy. "Orton was here. He threatened to send his version of our—our time together in Nice to the tabloids unless I fork over my office and an executive position."

"And?" Dolph could barely contain himself. His hands curled in expectation of having Orton's throat in their hold.

"I threw him out."

"Damn! I wanted to do that. I've been itching to give that stepbrother of yours the pounding he deserves." How many times over the years had he seen the triumph in Orton's eyes when he'd assured Dolph he didn't know Bedelia's whereabouts? "He's always known where you were, hasn't he?"

"Not at first." She swung away from the window, facing him. "He'll do what he says. He'll sell his story to someone."

Desire shot through Dolph. Her body was backlit by the setting sun, and her silhouette was fiery and curvy, desirable and beautiful. He wanted her badly. "Let him sell his story."

"Your career—"

"My career can take care of itself." Would she never learn that there was no contest when the choice was between her and his career? It would always be Bedelia. "I've weathered a few career storms in my time, and there'll be more. But will this hurt your business?"

She shrugged. "I don't think so. Who knows?"

"I won't let him hurt you."

Hope rushed through her soul. The sunlight

that speared over her shoulder etched his high cheekbones, outlined that strong jaw, and burnished his golden hair. "All you need is the horned helmet, Son of Wotan," she said softly.

"Just remember that Vikings made it a habit to win. And I'll take that twit stepbrother of yours apart if he comes near you again. I assume his executive's chair is empty."

All at once Bedelia laughed. "No, no, I'm not hysterical, Dolph. It's just that it paints such a picture."

Dolph took her in his arms, cuddling her close. "What picture?"

"You should have seen him," she said, struggling to control the tension-releasing mirth. "You should have seen Orton cartwheel out of that chair." She swallowed another giggle. "I hit him with the inkstand."

Keeping one arm around her, Dolph turned and picked up the inkstand. "I knew I liked this."

"And Lydia threatened him with a metal mailer." Laughter hiccuped out of her.

"A veritable army."

"Yes. You'd better beware, Wakefield."

"After we're married, I'll wear a suit of armor." He kissed her gently. "But tonight, like any newly engaged couple, we're going to celebrate."

She pulled back from him. "We are?"

"Yes." He quickly dialed a number, then turned on the speaker phone. Tightening his hold on her, he pulled her against his side. "Umm, it feels good to have you in my arms."

"Doesn't it." Bedelia closed her eyes. The longing and need had come flooding back. How she'd tamped it down for so long she didn't know. It had always been Dolph. He'd brought the sun up for her, made the moon shine. He'd been the impetus for her ambition, her need to succeed. Now he was here, holding her, wanting her. The world was sweet.

"Piers Larraby," a voice said over the speaker.

"It's Dolph. Could you and Damiene join us at the Carousel tonight? I'm going to call Bear and Kip too."

"We'll be there. They have a good band at the Carousel, don't they? I look forward to dancing with my wife . . . and Bedelia."

"Is that right?" Dolph drawled.

Piers laughed. "See you."

The phone clicked off, and Dolph looked at Bedelia ruefully. "He and Bear can usually read my mind about most things. And they know you mean a great deal to me."

"Do they?" Her heartbeat quickened.

"Yes. Now they know. For years they only suspected. I couldn't talk about it. You were buried too deep for them to see. But now they know." He kissed her forehead. "They can see it all because I can't hide it anymore."

Combing her fingers through his hair, she pulled his hand down to her. "I'm not hidden from you, nor will I ever be again," she said softly, and kissed him gently, once, twice. Then her lips clung to his, parting them.

Suspended in time, they held each other, swaying. Eons passed in seconds. Forever was theirs.

Dolph molded her to him, fitting her body to his as though he wanted to make them one. The kiss was the most intimate, erotic caress he'd ever shared, and all his body and soul pulsated into it.

A wondrous connection was made at that moment. Knowledge was a piercing light. He would always want her. Making love to her with his mouth was all the joy he could ever want. And there was so much more!

Bedelia was catapulted back to the joy of Nice. Dolph was happiness to her, as he'd always been. Kissing him was the most marvelous experience. She could have wept with delight.

Their mouths parted a fraction. Their breathing was ragged and loud. They opened their eyes and looked at each other.

His heart thudding against his breastbone, Dolph rested his forehead on hers. "Never, never will I let you leave me again."

"No." Her breath caught in her throat. Her laugh was low and hoarse. "You'd better show up at the church. I won't be left at the altar." She let him see her need, her want. She'd denied it for too long.

Heat and light exploded in him. Bedelia was his. He brushed his lips across her cheek. "I'll be there, at the church, waiting for you." He swept back the damp tendrils of hair that clung to her forehead. "Are you going to have someone give you away?"

She shook her head. "I'll walk down the aisle by myself. Be there." She looked up at him, allowing him to see the years of waiting in her eyes, the cold loneliness without him. Those years had been a wasteland. And she hadn't even known how desperately alone she'd been until now. Sorrow for the lost moments, grief for the unrequited affection, assailed her.

Dolph delved the shadows in her eyes, and his heart broke. She'd been his pain, and he'd been hers. His anger faded, and only love remained.

"I wouldn't miss watching you walk down the aisle for all the stars in the galaxy." His voice was uneven. When he saw the tears on her cheeks, he kissed them away. "Don't do that. I'll be crying." He dropped his mask forever. The ice that had frozen his emotions gave way with a roar inside him. "I'm yours, you know. I belong to you, Bedelia. And I have ever since I found you in my car in Nice. You took my life when you went away. Now you're here, and I want you to keep me."

Bedelia gulped and struggled with the emotion, but it had been dammed up so long. "Oh, Dolph . . . Dolph. I will. I will." The words were wrenched from her as grief and regret overwhelmed her. Tears of remorse cascaded down her cheeks, and she clutched him tightly.

"Those words are our vows, my love." His smile was shaky, but his eyes were steady. "I will keep you, my Bedelia, for all time."

They held on to each other.

"I never thought this would happen," she whispered. "I dreamed about it, but I was sure it couldn't work out. All my plans were for you, woven around you, but in my deepest soul I was afraid that I would be too late."

"You should have trusted me from the beginning, waif." He kissed her again, then lifted her and carried her to the couch. "I could make love to you now and not let you off this sofa until dawn." He smiled when he saw her blushing. "Why the red face, love? You must know how I feel."

"I'm blushing because you read my mind, Wake-field." She tapped his cheek with one finger. "I've had a few erotic thoughts about you these last years."

His eyes closed as though he'd had a sudden spasm of pain. "Stop. You're starting the wheels turning."

"Seeing a few visions yourself?"

"Yes, damn you," he said mildly, smiling when she laughed. He sat down, still holding her, set-tling her on his lap. "You're still tiny."

"I was never tiny." She touched his face with questing fingers. "You used to say that, but it wasn't true."

She saw the arrested look on his face. "You're back in Nice."

He nodded. "I'm watching you weed the garden, and there's dirt on your nose, perspiration has streaked dust across your face, and you have no makeup on."

"What a picture." She pretended to shudder.

"You're as beautiful in that garden as you are now, and I want you as much as I did then."

"Me too."

He looked down at her. "You were and are ador-able—and tiny." He kissed her deeply. "And I could make love to you forever."

She reached up and took his head in her hands, her mouth open on his, her tongue touch-ing his in mute declaration of love.

"I want you, Bedelia. Now."

"You'd get no argument from me . . . except you did say something about meeting people at The Carousel."

He winced, his head falling forward until it touched hers. "I've thought of another way to celebrate our engagement."

"And I can read your mind. But your friends . . ."

"I need to love you."

"The fact that you want to as much as I do allows me to be patient."

He kissed her searchingly, letting the passion he'd frozen melt into her. When he lifted his head, they were both struggling for air.

"Time . . . to go . . . ," she gasped.

Sighing, he stood up, still holding her.

"Put me down, Dolph, or we'll never leave."

"Right." He let her slide down his body.

She took his hand and led him toward the door. His words stopped her dead.

"Do you want children, Bedelia?"

She hesitated, then continued out of the office to the elevator. "Until I saw Patrick Dol-thus the other night, I might have answered maybe. After seeing him in action, I think I'd like a boy."

"I want a girl with red hair and violet eyes, who's spunky as hell."

"Like Tabitha."

"Yes."

The elevator sped them to the lobby. In minutes they were in his car. He didn't have a ticket.

"Would you mind if we stopped at my place first?" she asked. "I'd like to shower and change."

"So would I. We'll go to your place, then mine." He paused. "Will you stay with me tonight, Bedelia?"

"Yes."

"Thank God," he murmured.

He was able to park in front of her apartment building and followed her inside. They kissed again and again in the elevator.

When she went up the stairs to the second floor of her apartment, he called to her, "Anything I can help you with up there?"

She leaned over the banister and flashed him a smile. "Not yet."

Heat swept through him. She always smiled that way in Nice. "Sure you don't need me to scrub your back?"

Remembering all the times he did that in Nice weakened her knees and battered her good sense. "N-no," she said weakly.

Apparently she hadn't sounded convincing, for he started toward the stairs. "Are you sure?"

"Stay there, Dolph!" she ordered, then seeing the gleam in his eyes, sped up the stairs and into her bathroom.

Dolph pounded on the door as she locked it. "Bedelia! Dammit, I want to come in." His voice lowered. "I'll be good." Her laugh, low, husky, rippling, was like a match to his libido. "I promise."

"No, no, you wouldn't. You'd come in the shower with me, then we'd . . . make love . . . and go to bed . . ."

"Bedelia!" He hit the door with his fist. "And stop laughing."

"Would it help to know I am torturing myself by keeping you away?"

He leaned his head on the door. "A little, but not much."

His mutter made her laugh again, though she felt like groaning, felt like unlocking the door and casting herself into his arms. "We'd be too late, and your friends would know what we'd been doing and—"

"So what? If you knew how desperate they were to marry their wives, you'd realize they'd understand. I can't tell you the number of times I could barely keep their attention because they wanted each other so badly."

"I'll be out in a moment," she said regretfully.

"I'm going to shower in the other bedroom. A cold shower. Don't forget to pack the clothes you'll need for tomorrow." Grimacing, he turned away from the door.

"My nightie?"

That stopped him. Grinding his teeth, he faced the door again. "Bedelia, unless you want me to break down this door, stop being so provocative. You know damn well you won't be wearing anything." He stalked down the hall, muttering imprecations.

Bedelia sagged against the bathroom door. "He's turned me into a wet noodle, just by talking. It's definitely masochistic to marry him when I love him so much." She straightened. "But that's life. I can't live without him, so I'll bear my pain." She glared at the vanity mirror. "And stop talking to yourself."

When Bedelia joined Dolph in the sitting room,

she saw at once that his hair was damp from his shower.

He somehow looked both tense and relaxed.

He swung to face her. "You're driving me stark raving mad, wife-to-be."

She loved seeing him that way, humorous and edgy. "I'm a little wound up myself, but I don't mind." She shook her head. "There's no vacuum anymore . . . if you get my drift." She bit her lip to still its trembling.

"I do," he said quietly. "We broke through and connected." He extended his arm to her. "We'd better leave, because in ten seconds I'll be taking you back up those stairs and undressing you."

"We'd better hurry." Weak, she leaned on his arm.

At Dolph's home, he led her up to the door and unlocked it. When she would have entered, he stopped her, swinging her up into his arms. "This is your new home. And to me you're a bride," he said softly.

"Oh." Shaken, she could only clasp him tightly, her face pressed to his neck.

He paused in the front hall "Like your new home?"

She nodded.

"It's been in my family for generations, and I've tried to keep all the furnishings and decorations suitable to the Colonial period. If there's anything you'd like to change, or if you'd like to live elsewhere . . . ?"

She raised her head. Her cheeks were damp. "I like it here very much. I like the tradition. We can pass it on to our children. And if we want to change something, we'll decide together."

"Our children. That sounds wonderful." He kissed away the tears on her cheek. "I love you, Bedelia Fronsby. I have for a long, long time. And I don't see that changing down through the years."

"Better not try to get away from me, Wakefield. I'll track you down."

He frowned. "I wasn't the one who ran," he said, then cursed himself. He didn't need to remind her of that.

Would he ever forgive her? Bedelia wondered. She had the uneasy feeling it would take a long time. Maybe the rawness would never heal altogether. "Hadn't you better let me down? You have to get dressed."

He nodded and set her on her feet. "Feel free to explore the house. I'll be back shortly." Turning, he sprinted up the stairs.

Bedelia wanted to call him back to plead with him to try to understand why she'd left him, how she'd felt during the tough years that followed. Would he understand her driving desire to be on equal footing with him, to return to him as a peer?

She walked across the hall into the study and sat down, staring blindly at the floor-to-ceiling bookshelves.

All at once all the reasons that had sustained her since she'd run away from him seemed infantile, specious . . . and unnecessary.

Hiding her face in her hands, she sagged back into the leather chair. For ego, for pride, for stupidity, she'd put her life and Dolph's on hold for so many years. Why? Why hadn't she seen what was so clear now, what he'd seen right away? If they'd been together, they could have breasted any barriers, climbed any mountain. Pride had separated them, and it had been hers. They could have balanced things out together. They had always been equals! Love had made it so!

Stupid, stupid, stupid, she berated herself. No, they hadn't been equals on terms of skill, talent, experience. The equality between them had been opportunity, chance, and a desire to win it all.

"Damn, damn, damn!" she cried.

"What is it, Bedelia? What's wrong?" Dolph hurried across the room and knelt beside her chair. "Darling! You're pale. Has something frightened you?"

"Hold me, hold me," she said brokenly. "I was wrong, Dolph. I wasted so much."

He moved back from her so he could look into her eyes. "I know. I wondered when it would hit you. And I knew it would, waif. I know you too well."

"You do, do you?"

"Yes."

"I've done some soul-searching since we met again."

He pushed the hair back from her forehead. "Painful, isn't it?"

"Yes."

He kissed her cheeks. "We'll be all right. Do you have everything you need?"

"I will in a little while." She gazed into his eyes, letting the love and desire show.

He inhaled a shuddering breath "Let's go." He took her hand and whisked her out of the house. "We won't be separated anymore, darling. I promise."

She sighed and looked around the street. "I like this area. It doesn't seem like Manhattan, but like a small city in New England."

"I want you to like it here. We'll probably be in New York most of the time. But we have a home in California too, near Carmel." He touched her hand. "And I might try to see if I could purchase a certain villa in Nice. What do you think, partner?"

"Can we do that?"

"I'll do everything I can to get it."

"Wonderful."

Back in the car, he started driving north to the upper East Side. After a minute he said, "Bear asked me what parted us."

Electricity shot around the car.

"You can tell them it was my fault," Bedelia said. "False pride."

"It was mine," Dolph said. "I should have married you the second day I saw you."

Bedelia opened her mouth to scoff, then closed it again.

"It doesn't sound so crazy, does it?" he said softly.

"No. But I wonder if I was grown-up enough to see it."

"You were a little girl."

"My feelings about you weren't girlish."

Dolph's laugh was hoarse. "No. And you were all woman in my arms."

Bedelia trembled with need. Boneless with joy,

she could have slipped right off the seat. "By the way, shouldn't you tell me more about the wedding?"

"What?"

"Oh, like is it big or small, formal or informal? Do I know the witnesses, or are they strangers?"

"Darling, we're getting married. What difference does it make who's in it?"

"Witnesses, Dolph. It's the law."

He looked taken aback for a moment, then he winced. "I forgot."

"Why don't you ask Piers and Bear and Damiene and Kip?"

"I'd like that. Thank you."

"I like them very much, and their children are wonderful. No wonder you think of them as family."

He nodded. "They've been part of my life since shortly after we parted, and I sometimes think I couldn't have made it without them. Good people." He shot a glance at her. "You're not thinking of throwing me over because I didn't even remember we needed witnesses, are you?"

"You won't get away from me, Wakefield." And she meant it. Never again would she put the real living on hold. Dolph was life, and she needed him.

"Damn right." He kissed her hand, relief coursing through him. Not that he would have released her. He couldn't. If Bedelia ever rejected him, he wouldn't go. He'd do everything he could to change her mind, get back into her life. The first moment he saw her in Nice, he'd known that. And nothing had altered that powerful surge of truth.

"I was a fool to leave you," she murmured. "Those enobling thoughts I had were bogus, and they almost made dust of our lives. I will never put us in jeopardy again by repeating my stupid behavior. Do you believe me?"

He nodded, his throat clogged with emotion. "You make me warm again, lady. I may even cry."

"It must be catching," she said huskily. "Drive faster, but don't get a ticket."

"Yes, ma'am."

Seven

Bedelia walked out of the bathroom, ill at ease, unaccustomedly shy. All the warmth Dolph had engendered in her during the evening and on the ride home had dissipated.

The discomfort had begun when she'd told him after dinner that she wanted to pick up something at her apartment. His sharp glances and furrowed brow had unnerved her. For some reason, though, she couldn't tell him what she needed to get.

In her bedroom she'd retrieved from a drawer a frothy bit of diaphanous silk wrapped in blue tissue, its softness running through her hands like cream-colored water. She'd purchased the outlandishly expensive confection years ago in Paris, when she and Professor de Linde had had their first profitable year. She had never worn it.

When she returned to the car, Dolph had eyed the box, yet said nothing. In fact, words had all but died by the time they'd reached his front door.

She'd gone silently to the bedroom he'd indicated, separated from his by a sitting room.

When she'd donned the airy material, she stared at her body hazily outlined in silk. She wanted to be all things beautiful for Dolph.

Knowing she couldn't delay any longer, she crossed the bedroom and pushed open the door. Her hand was shaking, her heart pounding so hard, her ribs hurt. Her nerves were out of control. "Hi."

Dolph looked up from where he sat on a couch in front of the fireplace. His smile faded as he stood up. "Hi. When I used to run this scenario around my mind, I had a million speeches planned. But I've forgotten them all."

"Oh." Bedelia looked him up and down, admiring his silk pajamas. "I like that sea-green color on you. Very sexy." Her laugh was breathless.

"And you're devastating, darling." He reached out a hand, then dropped it to his side. "Don't be nervous."

"I can't help it. I've never seen you in pajamas before."

His own laugh was a trifle forced. "That's right." He stepped closer. "You're so beautiful."

"Why am I anxious? It's not our first time."

"Maybe it is." He saw the sheen of tears in her eyes and felt a moistness in his. "I love you, Bedelia Fronsby."

She nodded. "Thank you. I needed that." She reached out and took his hand, curling her fingers around his. "It means so much, doesn't it?"

"The two of us? Oh, yes, it means so much."
He touched the tie of the sheer negligee, tugging
gently until it fell open. His gaze roved over her
silk-clad body. "You still have the same luscious
curves that I loved to taste." He touched her lips
with one finger. "The first time. It will always be
the first time for us."

That touch went through her like a velvet
probe. She shuddered, her eyes closing. She was
a woman who'd mapped out her life, made tough
decisions, steered through the shoals of the business world. Tonight Dolph proved he was her real
destiny, and he'd done it with a feather-light
caress.

Her eyes opened. "This is ridiculous . . . but I'm
afraid."

He inched the negligee from her shoulders. "So
am I. It was never so important."

Her eyes widened. "You've had other women,
but I haven't had a man since you, Dolph." When
she saw the surprise in his eyes, she tried to
smile. "I don't want to mess up."

"Neither do I," he said huskily.

"That's silly." Her laugh was throaty and shaky.
When his hands furrowed through her hair, mas-
saging her scalp, her eyes closed again.

"No. You're so special to me, Bedelia." He drew
her closer.

At that moment Bedelia had a blindingly clear
perception that she and Dolph had been tied by
fate since the dawn of time. They'd been destined
to be together; the years they'd been apart had
been a teaspoon of sand in time. Yet even if this
would be only one night, it would truly be forever,

for Dolph possessed her, body, mind, and soul. She'd given herself to him in Nice.

She hadn't forgotten their time together, the moments when it had been hard to discern her body from his, the love-tangle of limbs and lips. The passion had been wild, wonderful, exhilarating.

She braced for the lightning strikes of fire that would ignite that passion. Instead, his lips brushed her in gentle questing, as though he'd given over the lead to her. He'd leave it to her to set the pace.

Surprised, she opened her eyes to find him watching her.

After a moment, she smiled. Leaning closer, she nipped his lower lip, delight racing through her when he shuddered.

Dolph wanted her with an elemental need, but he felt sublimely patient, willing to be still as she learned to trust him again. That was joy enough. His hands combed through her hair, the feel of it more erotic than anything he could recall. His control would be tested tonight because he wasn't going to rush anything.

Bedelia fumbled with a button on his pajama top. "You are formal tonight. I recall you wearing nothing." Confidence, with memory, was returning. Being with Dolph was passion, desire . . . and comfort. She'd had it all and would now have it again. She unbuttoned the jacket, letting one fingernail score down his hair-roughened chest.

"Excellent recall," he said as she pushed the jacket off his shoulders. When she toyed with his nipples, he couldn't stifle a groan.

"Annoying, isn't it," she said idly, "the way passion creeps up on one?" Happy, in control, she wanted to stretch every precious moment.

"Mine isn't creeping, it's galloping."

When she chuckled, her breasts rose and fell invitingly under the silk gown. He kissed one tantalizing curve.

When his lips slid up her neck to her cheek, she turned her head, her mouth open, catching his tongue with hers. His heartbeat accelerated so much, she could feel the pounding against her breasts. The beat became her own, and she pressed her body to his.

"Sweet, sweet," he murmured against her skin.

Then he swept her up into his arms and carried her into his bedroom. Setting her on her feet next to the bed, he sank down before her, kissing her middle, easing her back onto the bed.

Bedelia didn't even feel her knees give way. It was as though she'd floated down onto the silken coverlet.

Then they were supine, holding each other, breathing into each other's mouths, alive again because they were together, needing and wanting.

Bedelia shivered as he slipped her gown off. Could it be as wonderful as before? She wondered, suddenly uncertain.

Dolph misunderstood her shiver, and slipped her under the covers. "I'll keep you warm, always," he promised.

She touched his face. "I wasn't cold. Just excited."

Her fingers seemed to burn his skin, igniting a sensual fire within him. He shed the rest of his pajamas and pressed his body to hers, kissing her passionately.

Bedelia's being flowered. Once before she'd known his love, exulted in it. It should have been the same . . . but it was so much more. Dolph took her through a veritable paradise island for lovers, a winding, sweet new path to love.

She arched and gasped beneath him. Her skin was so sensitized to him, it quivered with life. She could smell, touch, and taste him, and she wanted more. All of her senses heightened as he kissed her breasts, her shoulders, her knees, her feet. She cried out when he gently caressed her throat.

Tasting his tongue was old and new. His urgent tutoring was a memory, as was the sleek sliding of his body over hers. She tensed for the buildup she knew was coming, her body swaying as it caught the rhythm of their love. Gasping, she gave in to the tide that whirled her closer to him, as his hand skimmed up her thigh to find her moistness.

She fought for air as Dolph took it all . . . and gave it back. He eased into her body, finding her tight and ready for him.

She clung to him, her nails digging in as he swept her beyond her control.

They took each other with a passion that shattered all their memories. Had there ever been such giving?

Together they climbed to the summit of their love, higher . . . higher . . . higher. Until the explosion of ecstasy.

In the sweet aftermath there was a shuddering

silence. One breath was like a thunderclap as, sated, they returned to earth.

Conversation would have been an intrusion. A finger touch was enough.

Time rolled away in sweet minutes.

Bedelia had known what to expect, or at least she'd thought so. Dolph's beautiful loving had lived in her heart since Nice. Why had it shattered her now? It had been revolutionary, awesome. And she'd been changed irrevocably.

Dolph pressed her close to him. He wanted to love her again and again, to cherish her and keep her. Belonging to her completely was all the happiness he needed. Not work, not people, not places could ever intrude on that.

Sleep came like a soft blanket, covering, comforting.

The night darkened to deep black, studded with stellar fairy lights. Then it faded to shades of gray, until orange rayed the night sky, signaling dawn.

Bedelia awoke and turned in Dolph's arms, rested and replete, happy in the special homecoming of his love.

He smiled at her. "I like watching you sleep." She excited him yet soothed him. She was of exotic beauty, but earthy and simple.

"Do you?" He was so exciting in the morning, she mused. So sensual. His mussed hair was a particular stimulus, and she wanted it for all time. He looked vulnerable and powerful, boyish, and virile.

"Last night was wonderful, Bedelia."

"It was, wasn't it?"

"I want to make sure we don't forget it." With powerful hands he lifted her over him. Her hair cascaded over them, imprisoning them in soft drifting curtains. "I'm going to want to love you all the time, Bedelia Fronsby."

Passion built in her even as she laughed. "If you're waiting for protests, forget it," she said throatily. Shifting herself, she fitted over him. "I can see you're in tune with me." She moved again.

"Darling! Bedelia!"

Passion took them again, and they gasped at its power.

By the time they rose from the bed and showered—which took a long time, because they began caressing each other again—they were both late.

"I had an appointment with Welmer an hour ago," Dolph said, smiling when she chuckled.

"Lydia will be pulling out her hair," she said dreamily.

"Better go." Dolph didn't move. "Of course, we might as well be really late. You could cancel your morning appointments. I could tell Welmer to suck an egg." Her dimples flashed, and desire exploded in him. "What do you say to a little fence painting, Tom-Sawyer style?"

She clapped her hands and threw her head back, laughing. "I say we're crazy and we can't get away with it." Her head snapped back down, and she grinned at him. "Let's do it, Wakefield."

He grabbed her, whirling her around. "That's my waif of the night."

"Put me down, I'm dizzy."

"First we'll go to your house, and I'll get some

of Lorette's wonderful coffee while you get your sports bag."

"Racquetball?"

"Swimming. It won't be the sea, but we have imaginations."

"If I go to a pool, I won't envision us in the sea. Most of the time we were naked."

"Umm, I remember." He caressed her back, his mouth trailing over her shoulder and neck.

Bedelia pushed back from him, out of breath. "We'll never leave here."

"Spoilsport. I was just getting started."

She giggled, then clamped her hand over her mouth.

"I like that sound, you know," he whispered.

Only by great force of will did they break apart.

Outside Bedelia gazed at the blue sky, inhaled the crisp air, and laughed out loud. "Perfect."

"Isn't it?" He kissed her and helped her into the passenger seat of his car.

When he slipped under the wheel, she was staring at him. "What is it?" he asked.

"You're a Viking in Giulianis. And I could eat you up."

He almost lifted her over the console when he kissed her. "Stop laughing when I'm loving you. You did that in Nice."

"I can't help it. I'm having such fun."

The drive through Manhattan was glorious. It was their kingdom, and they were alone in it.

"Dolph, do you want us to live in California?"

He shook his head. "Your business is here. We'll work out of New York. Sometimes you can come on location with me."

"Sometimes? Uh-uh. All the time."

"Yeah."

When they reached her apartment building, they hurried into the elevator, kissing and hugging.

The doors opened, and Lorette stood there, arms akimbo. "You did not call, Mademoiselle. Fawns-bee. This is not good. I—" Then she saw Dolph. "M'sieur! Now I know where she was. You should have called me, m'sieur."

"Lorette. It's good to see you. I'm sorry. It won't happen again."

Lorette shrugged. "Of course I'm glad you are here." She eyed Bedelia. "She was ill for you, m'sieur. *Mal d'amour.*"

Dolph chuckled.

Bedelia glared at her housekeeper. "You're fired."

"Soon M'sieur will be the boss," Lorette said. "Then we'll see. Are you eating?"

"No, we're swimming." He patted Bedelia on the backside. "See. After we're married, you'll know who's boss."

"Why you—you sexist . . ."

He sprinted for the stairs and she darted after him.

Lorette watched them race the stairs and shook her head. "You still play like children. Shame on you."

They left the apartment much later, arms around each other and Dolph carrying Bedelia's sports bag. In the car she abruptly turned to him.

"I wanted you to know that there were no other men in my life. Just you."

Red crawled up his neck.

"I didn't say that to embarrass you, Dolph. I just wanted you to know."

"I'm not embarrassed. I'm delighted." He swallowed. "You know I've had other women. But you were always there, Bedelia. I couldn't commit to anyone because you had my love and I couldn't get it back."

She sighed, leaning back against the seat. "I'm glad."

"So am I."

"I saw *Frozen Idol* five times," she said softly.

"I wrote it for you."

She cried then, because she was happy . . . and sorry for what they'd lost.

"I needed you then," he murmured, "and I need you now."

She leaned over and kissed him.

Eight

The days that followed were chaotic and wonderful.

Bedelia was sure her staff thought she'd run mad. Dolph was either in her office or on the phone with her. Not that she cared what anyone thought. She was in a special cocoon with him, and she didn't want it to change. She'd never known such delight, such freedom from care.

Sometimes she had hour-long conference calls with Damiene Larraby and Kip Kenmore, consulting with them about the wedding gown the French designer Charine was creating for her. With a wrench she realized how much she'd missed the "girl" thing that she hadn't had time for in her climb up the ladder.

Lydia was alternately delighted with the upcoming nuptials and frustrated by Bedelia's dreamy, nonchalant attitude toward it.

"I wish you'd at least look at the flower list,"

she said one morning, chewing her lip. "Tomorrow's the day. Why should I be so nervous and not you?"

"I don't know." Bedelia smiled benignly, picking up her phone when it rang before Lydia could. "What? The driver for the wedding?" She put her hand over the phone. "Something else Dolph forgot to tell me, I'll bet." She giggled.

Lydia rolled her eyes, taking the phone from her. "I'll handle it." She spoke into the phone. "You were saying? Ah, yes, the driver for the wedding."

"I'm getting married tomorrow," Bedelia informed her secretary.

"I know that," Lydia said from the side of her mouth. "Go ahead, please. You were saying about the driver . . ."

"I think we're supposed to pick up Damiene and Kip," Bedelia said helpfully. "And maybe the driver could pick us up after our fitting tomorrow morning. This is the time." She scribbled on a piece of paper and tried to press it into her secretary's hand.

"Wait a minute, will you?" Lydia snapped. "I'm talking on the phone." Her jaw dropped when she realized how she'd just spoken to her employer.

"Okay." Bedelia's smile widened.

Lydia rolled her eyes again. "I'll never get through this. No, no, I'm not talking to you," she said into the phone. "Would you repeat that, please? Yes, the name of your company, and what you'll be doing for Miss Fronsby and her party." She took a pen from Bedelia's desk and turned a scratch pad toward her. "You're Gotham Limousine. Yes, I have that. And you'll be picking up Miss Fronsby—"

"And Mrs. Kenmore and Mrs. Larraby," Bedelia added again.

"I'll tell them that," Lydia muttered. "Yes, yes, I'm listening. And you can pick them up at Charine's on Fifth Avenue?"

"We should be done by eleven o'clock," Bedelia said.

Lydia coughed and repeated what Bedelia had said. "That's correct. I guess we're all set. Thank you." Lydia put down the phone and sighed. "I hope I get through this."

"You will. You'll dance at my wedding."

Lydia laughed reluctantly. "I've never, ever seen you this way."

"Happiness does it to you."

Bedelia went back to work when her secretary left, but more than once she caught herself smiling and thinking about Dolph.

That night, as they'd done since Bedelia had moved in with Dolph a week earlier, they sat with their arms around each other after dinner, smiling, talking a little, listening to music.

"Tomorrow at this time we'll be flying to Europe, sweetheart." Dolph nibbled on her ear. "Of course, we won't have Lorette there with us, but we'll have our place."

"Oh, Dolph, I can't believe the villa's ours. It means so much." She nuzzled her face into his neck. "Umm, I'm not sure I'll ever want Lorette to accompany us there."

Dolph laughed and pulled her closer.

That night they made love with a serene frenzy that left them reeling.

The next day, Dolph woke her with a kiss. "Hey, sleepyhead. I thought you needed to go for a fitting for your gown."

Bedelia smiled, her eyes still closed. Then she opened them and glanced at the clock. Yelping, she tried to jump out of the bed.

Dolph held her fast. "Not yet. I need to kiss you good morning while you're still Miss Fronsby."

"I'll be late for my fitting," she said weakly, holding him to her. "And I'm meeting Kip and Damiene there."

Her lips against his cheek set him on fire. He pressed his mouth to hers, the kiss deepening instantly.

"You said a kiss," she murmured shakily when he released her.

"I lied."

"Awful man." She breathed in his essence, clutching him, wanting him.

"*Your* man." She excited him as no one else ever had, Dolph thought, but even as the blood pounded through him, he felt more at peace than at any other time. She both soothed and aroused him. And if the nightmare of being parted from her still haunted him, it lasted only a short time.

"My man," she whispered. She rubbed her bare leg against his, then closed her eyes in delight as he began to caress her body with his lips.

By the time Bedelia finally did get out of bed, it was almost time for her fitting.

"I'll call Charine and tell her to work with Damiene and Kip first," Dolph said, grinning.

"Lecher." He hooked an arm around her waist as she tried to pass him and kissed her deeply. "Hurry home. I need to marry you."

She looked straight into his eyes. "I love you, Adolphus Prentice Wakefield. And I can't wait to be your wife." Before he could gather her close again, she was out of the bedroom and racing to the stairs.

"Hey, not fair!" He jumped out of bed, ran out to the hall, and looked over the banister. "You shouldn't say such provocative things to me, then skip away. And don't run down the stairs like that. You could've fallen." He grimaced when she laughed and threw him a kiss.

Luck was with her. She got a taxi at once, and the driver was able to maneuver through the crush of Manhattan traffic so that she wasn't too awfully late.

Almost at once she was swept into the sanctum sanctorum of the tiny, world-famous couturiere.

"Ah, Mademoiselle Fawns-bee," Charine greeted her. "That man Wakefield keeps you late. I know this. He is much man. Yes?"

"*Oui.*" Dolph was all the men in the world.

Charine laughed gently when her customer looked sheepish. "Be glad you have such a man." A small shudder went over her tiny frame. "Some men can be such bores."

Damiene and Kip, who'd come from another fitting area, heard the last remark and laughed.

"You laugh because you have such men," Charine said, shrugging in a very Gallic fashion. "But all women are not so lucky." She gestured to all three women. "Come, I will have you all with your gowns on. Mademoiselle Fawns-bee will need more work, but I think you two are fine."

In very little time the three women were pirouetting in front of Charine in the large fitting room.

Soon Charine had dismissed Kip and Damiene.

"We'll meet you at the church," Kip said, grinning. "I'm getting nervous. And I wasn't, at my own."

Damiene closed her eyes. "Why did you have to say that?"

"Don't forget the children," Bedelia said, smiling at her two new friends. She liked Damiene and Kip very much and was entranced with their progeny.

"You might be sorry." Kip said, and grimaced when her friends laughed.

Once Bedelia was alone with Charine, the designer didn't waste any time. Bedelia was pinned, pushed, draped, and turned every which way.

"A tuck here and there," Charine finally pronounced, "and it will be perfection. Of course. I will have it sent to you, Mademoiselle Fawns-bee. It will be there before you. A Frenchwoman will be there to receive it? That's good. I have spoken with her on the phone."

"Lorette," Bedelia said. "Yes, she's wonderful. Thank you for everything, Charine."

"*Pas du tout, mademoiselle. Bonne fortune. Au'voir.*"

Bedelia was in a daze when she walked out to

Fifth Avenue. Before she could hail a cab, she saw a black Cadillac with a sign in the front passenger window. Gotham Limousine Service, she mused. Fuzzily she recalled the phone call the previous day. Had the driver returned Kip and Damiene to their homes? She waved to him, and he gestured for her to get in.

"This was a good idea," she said as she settled on the back seat. "I might have had trouble finding a cab."

The driver nodded and pulled into traffic.

Bedelia leaned back and closed her eyes. That very day she would become Bedelia Fronsby Wakefield. Wonderful! She'd waited so long. Sometimes she feared their wedding would never happen. Shaking her head, she drove away the black thoughts. Today was her wedding day. She indulged herself by daydreaming about Dolph.

When the car stopped, then began inching forward through the heavy traffic, she told herself not to worry. She still had plenty of time. She said a little prayer there wouldn't be any gridlock.

When the driver turned down a side street, she figured he was trying to avoid some congestion. No need to fret. There was plenty of time.

The cab wove in and out of so many streets, heading south and west, Bedelia soon was lost. When she saw the Hudson River, she frowned. They'd gone pretty far out of the way.

"Driver, I do have to get to my destination fairly soon. And it seems we've gone too far west."

"It's all right, ma'am. I know the way."

"All right." She settled back, her mind drifting once more to Dolph.

A few minutes later the car stopped. Bedelia sat up and looked around. A dock! "Driver, look—"

"Time to get out." He got out of the car and turned to open her door.

"You!" she exclaimed when she saw the man's face. "What on earth are you doing, Orton? Why are we here? And why are you driving a cab?"

"So many questions, dear sister. This isn't a cab. It's my car. I'm Gotham Limousine, a made-up company just for the occasion. I'm the one who called and talked to you and your secretary yesterday. It was a simple ploy, and it caught you. Your secretary never even checked on Gotham Limousine. She just assumed it was legit. Maybe she figured you or your sweetie had done the arranging." He laughed and reached in, grabbing her arm and pulling her from the car.

Bedelia recalled how she'd assumed Dolph had set up the limousine service. Hadn't she said something like that to Lydia? "I don't like this one bit, Orton, and I don't think it's funny." She faced him in the deserted area, trying to pull free.

"I don't care what you think." He pinched her arm.

At first she was too dumbfounded to react. Then she pushed at him angrily.

"Don't make a fuss, Bedelia. Just come with me. This gun is real."

She looked from his face to his hand, incredulous. "What are you doing? I'm getting married this afternoon and—"

"Not until you sign over Delia Cosmetics to me," Orton said grimly.

Bedelia smothered her first inclination, which

was to tell him to go to hell. "Orton, you know I couldn't do that today, even if I tried. The board would have to be convened—"

"I have a paper that you'll sign, then you can go on your way and get married to that papier-máché macho man you slept with in Nice."

Bedelia steeled herself against recoiling. She saw hatred in his eyes, not just the malicious spite she'd grown used to.

Fear was a hard lump inside her.

Dolph went to the phone five times to call Bedelia that afternoon, but he didn't do it. She would be busy dressing. He wished he had arranged to dress at her place. He wanted to be near her.

At one o'clock Bear and Piers strolled into his bedroom, grinning.

"He's nervous," Bear said in fake sympathy. "Hey, Dolph, we've all felt it. I was sure Kip would bolt on me and . . ." His voice trailed off when Dolph's expression hardened. "What is it?"

"I don't know. Nothing. Nerves, I guess." She'd run from him in Nice, and his life had been one hell after another.

Piers frowned, settling himself on a chair. "Call her if you're jumpy. Talk to her for a minute and put your mind at ease."

Dolph hesitated. "I wanted to do that, but I was afraid I'd disturb her while she was getting ready."

Bear shrugged. "Chances are, she wants to talk to you. Nerves are funny things." But he frowned at Piers as Dolph strode to the phone.

"What's up?" Piers murmured to Bear.

"Nothing gets to him. Nothing ever has. Now he's like a cat on a hot griddle."

Piers nodded slowly, exhaling. "You're right. Something's going on in that head of his. Nerves. It's got to be nerves." But his eyes narrowed on his friend.

"Lorette? It's Dolph. May I speak to Bedelia? What? No, she isn't here. I'm dressing here, but she was going back to her place to get ready. Easy, calm down, Lorette. There's been no accident, just a minor delay, I'm sure. You take care of the dress. Bedelia should be along at any moment."

His face icy still, Dolph hung up, then quickly dialed another number. "Charine? Dolph Wakefield." The conversation was short and to the point. When Dolph hung up, he stared at his two friends. "She left there well over an hour ago." He inhaled deeply. "Something's wrong. I should have followed my instincts and called before." He hit the palm of one hand with his fist. "Damn! What happened?"

Piers went to him. "She wanted this. So something's keeping her from it. You know that."

"Piers is right," Bear said firmly.

Dolph nodded. "I know. But something's holding her up. And I want to know what it is." The phone rang, and he grabbed it. "Shim? Where is she? Thanks for calling. I'm going myself. No, I think I know who it is. From your description it's her stepbrother Orton. Though I don't know why the hell he should have taken her there."

Dolph hung up the phone. "Stay here," he told

Piers and Bear. "Shim's going to call back. One of his people noticed that a black car followed Bedelia this morning. So he watched. Sure enough, the black car was parked in front of Charine's, a sign on it that said Gotham Limousine. Bedelia got in. He drove her down to the docks on the Hudson."

"Dolph, look at me," Piers said quietly. "You stay here and we'll go. We don't want you killing him."

"I'm getting her back," Dolph said. "I lost her once. I won't ever again."

"Don't kill anyone, Dolph," Bear said, gently serious. "Today's your wedding day. You take somebody out on this day, and it won't look good at the fiftieth anniversary party."

"Bear's right, Dolph. You know it."

Dolph nodded. He stripped off the morning suit he'd just donned, and grabbed a sweatshirt and jeans. "I'm marrying Bedelia. Today. Nothing will get in the way of that. Wait for Shim's call." He threw on his clothes and bolted from the room.

Bear shut his eyes and pressed one hand to his forehead. "He knows who has her, and he's going to kill him."

Piers sighed. "We'll have to rely on his good judgment." He shook his head. "But, dammit, I wouldn't blame him. I know what it feels like. So do you."

Bear nodded soberly. "I'll call Kip. She and Damiene can get to the church and put a lid on things. Then we'd better contact Shim Locke and find Dolph."

"I hope he can hang onto his temper."

"Nobody could call him the Frozen Idol now."

Bedelia walked down the long pier, the area alien to her. She could see the Statue of Liberty, but the lady certainly couldn't do her any good. She felt numb, as though she stood outside herself and were watching a play unfold. She ignored that sensation. Doing something to protect herself and getting to Dolph was prime in her mind. But what?

"Get moving," Orton ordered, "and don't bother trying anything, Bedelia. I chose this pier because few people use it. I doubt there's anyone around who'd hear you if you screamed. That might anger me, anyway. And someone could get hurt."

Taking a deep breath, she stopped and faced him. "I don't care if you get angry. You're a fool, Orton." She didn't flinch when he brandished the gun. She recalled from their childhood days that Orton often bullied children smaller than he, but he could be intimidated by his peers. "Listen to me. Even if I sign a piece of paper saying that you own my share of Delia Cosmetics, there's no guarantee the board will accept it. There is a system of checks and balances to prevent such exigencies. Every good company has them."

She bit her lip at the angry glitter in his eyes. He'd looked like that the time he'd held her under water. If his mother hadn't gotten to him, he might have drowned her. Bedelia remembered how her stepmother had hugged her and cried. Had she known then that her son had tried to kill Bedelia? Bedelia closed her eyes in sudden pain. Whatever Orton lacked as a human being, it had been gone for a long time. Maybe if he'd had help . . . Why hadn't her parents . . . ?

"That's why you're going to give me a cashier's check," Orton said, "and a signed affidavit that Delia Cosmetics is mine." He gestured to her to keep moving toward a boat at the end of the dock. "Get on board, Bedelia. It's not a big boat, but it's ocean-going and it'll do the job."

She stiffened at his tone. Her life was truly in danger! To stand still and be intimidated would get her nothing. Attacking him could get her nothing as well . . . or everything. She glanced at the dark, cold water. Though the early autumn air had a sticky warmth to it, the water would be ice-cold. Still there could be a chance that way. Orton had always been overly confident that his most outrageous schemes would work . . . but they'd always been flawed in some way. His newest plan might have some holes, some weakness she could use to her own advantage. Concentrate!

At his prodding she crept down the hatchway into a good-size cabin.

She blinked at the brightness when he switched on the light. "How long have you had this?" she asked. She didn't give two hoots what he had or for how long, but she needed time to decide what to do.

Why had she been so stupid? she wondered. Why hadn't she seen that Orton could be dangerous? Even as she asked herself the questions, the notions seemed absurd. People didn't have predators in their families. That was for television, made-up stories.

Orton smiled. "I haven't owned the boat for long, but I've used it many times. I bought it secondhand with your credit card, dear sister. It should be on this month's statement. I've used your credit-card number before, but this is the largest purchase I've made. All the other times I've been careful not to purchase too much, so it wouldn't be suspicious. And I've always been able to forge your signature when the occasion arose." He frowned. "Your accounting people are lax. When I'm in charge, that will change."

Bedelia stared at him. It was as though he didn't really know she was there but was operating on a different plane. His eyes glittered strangely; there was a tic at the corner of his mouth. Had she ever known him?

His smile widened. "So you were going to marry today. And I wasn't invited. Tch, tch. What would Mummy and Daddy think?"

Bedelia blinked at the sudden ferocity in his voice. "I don't know what they'd think, Orton."

"Don't you?" he said savagely. "You were their darling, the one they loved." He glared at her. "My own mother doted on you. And she was always there, protecting her darling whenever I got too close." The tic worsened. "I should've gotten half that money. Instead, it all went to you." A bubble of spittle appeared at the corner of his mouth.

"That money came from my own mother, Orton, and had nothing to do with you. It had been my mother's legacy from her father, and my father stipulated it should go to me. Besides, it was barely enough to get me started on my schooling, not a fortune as you always implied."

His face twisted. "You've always lied to me. So did they." He looked around. "I should tie you up. I want to get under way."

Bedelia froze. If he tied her and then left the harbor, her chances of escaping would drop alarmingly. No one would know where she was, what had happened. Dolph would believe she'd disappeared again, that she didn't love him. The thought sickened her. She had to think. Her best chance of getting back to Dolph was now. Think!

"I was glad when they died, you know," Orton went on. "Your father wanted to put me away. My mother would've let him." He banged his free hand against the bulkhead.

Blood congealed in her veins. "I didn't know." She edged closer to the bulkhead. There was a small fire extinguisher there.

"Let's go. I'm taking you topside with me while I get under way. I'll tie you up there. I'm not taking my eyes off you until I get my money." He gestured with his gun toward the gangway.

Bedelia didn't point out that she had little money with her, and only her personal checkbook, not the business one. She blessed the fact he wasn't going to tie her in the cabin. But she had to do something before he could put a rope on her.

Preceding him up the gangway, she looked around frantically, searching for a weapon.

In the wheelhouse she spotted another fire extinguisher. Orton was standing behind the wheel, studying the instruments, though his gun was trained on her.

She moved slowly toward the extinguisher, turning her body so it hid it. One hand inched back toward the fitting, groping, searching, then yanking the extinguisher free of the holder.

With all of her strength she threw it at him.

A motion, maybe an instinct, warned him. He brought up his hands, but the force of the extinguisher hitting him was enough to throw him off balance.

Bedelia was running as she heard him gasp in pain. She saw the gun drop, but she didn't try to retrieve it. Putting distance between herself and Orton was uppermost on her mind.

"Damn . . . you . . . Bedelia."

His cursing followed her as she jumped to the deck and raced to the stern. From there she leapt to the dock.

She was running full tilt when she heard the first shot. Cringing, she tried to increase her speed, even as he came pounding after her.

She had almost reached flat ground. The road to the main avenue was in sight.

Orton tackled her, he took her down to the hard dock.

Her head struck the wood, and her mind went black.

Nine

Dolph responded like an automaton. He took a cab because it was quicker, handing the driver a hundred-dollar bill. "There's double that if you can move."

"Right." The driver's smile died when he looked at his customer's face. The momentary familiarity of the visage had disappeared. He'd never seen that rock-hard killer look. "Where to?"

Dolph gave directions, checked the revolver he'd taken from his desk, and tried to repress thoughts of the many things that could already have happened to Bedelia.

The drive through Manhattan was the worst experience he'd ever known. Tension was a pressure that expanded to the point of explosion. He cursed steadily and fluently in three languages when he wasn't sending up streams of prayers. Spare Bedelia! Whatever else happened.

By the time they'd reached the approximate

location described by Shim Locke's operative, Dolph was thanking all the stars for the studio's insistence on having Shim Locke watch him all these years. If it hadn't been for that, he might never have been able to find Bedelia. Even so he could be too late.

Hopping out of the cab, he handed the driver another hundred-dollar bill. "If I'm not back here in an hour, call the police and get them here."

The driver turned off his car and stepped out. "I'll go withya, Mac. I can handle myself pretty well."

Dolph smiled briefly. "I don't doubt it. Stay here. You can help me better that way."

The driver nodded. "But if I hear anything strange, I'll phone it in and be right behindya."

Dolph was already gone, running fast along the pier until he spotted a boat moored by itself at the end of a dock. His instincts told him that was the boat. He ran even faster—then stopped dead.

Bedelia leapt off the boat onto the dock, her face tight and determined. He was about to call out to her when he saw Orton jump onto the dock in close pursuit. Dolph was running at the same time—mute, angry, frightened he wouldn't be able to reach her.

Then Orton tackled her.

Dolph raced toward her, fear and fury pumping the adrenaline through him. Bedelia!

Orton saw him as he was scrambling to his feet, the gun dangling by his side. Then the gun came up, pointing at the back of Bedelia's head.

"I'll shoot her, you know," Orton said conversationally.

Dolph stopped, hands hanging loose. He took deep steadying breaths to mask his panic. "Why? You can have what you want by asking. Name it. Money? We both have plenty, and you're welcome to it."

Orton's face screwed into adolescent pique. He swung the gun wildly, then fixed it again on Bedelia. "She took what was mine."

"Dolph."

Bedelia's whisper reached him, but he didn't look at her. "Then we'll give it back." He balanced on the balls of his feet. He wasn't close enough to ensure getting Orton if he leapt at him. Bedelia was still in danger.

"Don't patronize me!" Orton's scream of outrage startled some herring gulls that had been floating along the river. Their answering cries of protest had the same high-pitched decibels as Orton's.

Dolph readied himself as the other man jerked Bedelia to her feet. He shook when he saw the cut on her neck, the glazed look on her face. His hands flexed. Forcing the bile back down his throat, he spoke calmly. "You'll get more if you cooperate. People know you're here."

Orton glanced around furtively, fear making his movements jerky. "I'll kill her if you don't get out of the way. Then you can take her body out of the river."

Dolph took a step backward.

Bedelia watched his face intently, feeling the prod of the gun at the back of her head. "Dolph, don't—"

"Easy, darling. Everything is fine." He didn't take his eyes off Orton.

"Hey, you with the gun!" The cabbie yelled from behind Dolph. "I called the cops!"

The momentary interruption was enough. The gun wavered. Dolph moved.

He shot past Bedelia, grabbing Orton's hand, lifting it, pointing the gun skyward.

The two men struggled, swaying, the gun wavering.

Bedelia watched the gun, murmuring Dolph's name over and over, barely aware of the man behind her yelling that he was coming.

The gun fired.

Bedelia saw Dolph wince and pull back. Then he was at Orton again. She tried to maneuver to help him. Fear overwhelmed her, so that she scarcely heard the noises behind her.

"No! No!" she screamed suddenly.

Both men hesitated at her shrill cries. Then Dolph shoved Orton, and the other man went down. He swung toward Bedelia. "Tell me. Were you hit?"

"No." She flung herself at him, gripping him tightly, gulping back the tears. "Dolph, Dolph. You're hit. I saw you flinch."

Orton scrambled backward, frustration and fear warring over his features. Jumping to his feet, he ran back to the boat.

The dock shook as the cabbie ran toward them. "Help's coming."

Men in uniform and in plainclothes burst onto the pier. Bedelia saw that Bear and Piers were with them. Then the boat roared to life, reversing rapidly out into the river.

Dolph pushed her behind him, covering her body with his, his gaze on the boat as it headed out of the harbor.

A policeman stopped beside them, slipping his gun back into his holster. "I hope he isn't going to head down the coast. They're predicting that hurricane is going to hit the South tonight."

Dolph pulled Bedelia close to him. "He's at full throttle. Maybe you'd better contact the Coast Guard."

The policeman nodded and walked away.

"I'm glad you're all right, Dolph," Shim Locke said. He almost cracked a smile.

"He's not all right. He was hit." Neither Shim nor Dolph acknowledged her remark.

"Thanks for having her followed. I wouldn't have found her for a while if you hadn't." Dolph shook with recalled terror. Then he looked down at her. "I can't believe I have you, Bedelia Fronsby."

"Soon to be Wakefield, I hope," she said shakily, feeling very teary when she saw the hint of moistness in his eyes. "But only if we go to the hospital, this minute and you get some first aid."

He kissed her. "I assure you that it's nothing compared to the wound I received when I knew you'd disappeared."

"But now I'm here, Dolph."

"Hey, you two, don't we have a wedding?" Bear asked. He was grinning, but he stared at Bedelia searchingly.

"I think we do." Piers's smile didn't totally hide his anxiety. "Are you all right, Bedelia?"

"Yes, to both questions," she said huskily. "I'm afraid I'm a little the worse for wear right now, but my dress will be at the house, and I can change in a hurry. Then we'll—"

"I'm taking you to the hospital first," Dolph said tersely. "She has a gash below her jaw." When he'd seen Orton tackle her, ice had flowed through him. She could have broken her neck.

"It's just a scratch. I'll put some antiseptic on it, and I'll be fine." Bedelia herself was slightly alarmed at Dolph's pallor, and he seemed unnaturally stiff. His lips appeared clenched over his teeth. "You're the one who has to be checked."

He ignored that. "We can't be sure you didn't harm yourself, Bedelia. You hit that dock pretty hard. Damn him for doing this to you." He kissed her cheek. He could hardly believe he had her back.

She shook her head in pained wonder as she stepped into his arms. "He was wild, Dolph. I've never seen him that way."

"You were damned brave. I saw how you ran from him." And to Dolph she had seemed a million miles away from his protective grasp.

She looked at her love, her mouth trembling. "All these years I thought my parents weren't aware of Orton's actions. He told me they'd wanted to have him confined." She exhaled a shuddering sigh. "I never thought he was mentally ill, but he must be."

"It's over now, love. I promise." Dolph gazed over her head at his friends. "I want to get her into the cab and to the hospital. She's chilled through."

Piers nodded, smiling at Bedelia.

"Your cab driver is quite a boy," Bear said, "When we came down the road, he turned like a bull on the charge. Formidable." He chuckled as he led Bedelia along the pier. "Come on, little lady, let's hustle. We've got to get you to the church, somewhat on time."

Bedelia nodded, realizing that Dolph wanted to speak to Piers out of her hearing. But what was Dolph saying to Piers?

"The man in the boat is her stepbrother," Dolph said.

Piers whistled soundlessly. "And you want him found and put on ice. Right?"

"I won't have him near Bedelia again. He's done enough to her, Piers, maybe more than I know, or than she remembers. But I do recall the first time we were swimming together—she was terrified when I took hold of her in the water. It was as though she had to fight against me, as though I was trying to drown her." Dolph grimaced. "I was a fool not to have probed more deeply into what happened with her and her stepbrother."

"Did you know he was in this country?"

Dolph shrugged angrily. "Yes. He went to her office and made caustic noises because we were together again. Bedelia didn't want a fuss, and I went along with it. I damn well should have argued with her." Eyes anguished, he stared at his friend. "We've talked all around him, mentioned him, but never once did it occur to me he was a real danger to her."

"Easy." Piers put his hand on his friend's arm. Dolph nodded, then hurried to Bedelia's side.

"Couldn't stay away, huh?" Bear asked.

"No." Dolph pulled her into his arms, kissing her gently, then he led her to the cab.

Neither spoke until they were on the way to the hospital. Then Dolph pulled her close, his face in her hair. "Don't scare me that way anymore. You're enough of a thrill to me. I don't need any others."

She smiled into his shoulder. "Oh, Dolph, I was so glad to see you." She lifted her head. "What were you and Piers discussing?"

He sighed, kissing her again. "I want them to find Orton and turn him in, and they can do it with Shim Locke's help." He touched her cheek. "You know I have to do this."

Bedelia nodded. "I should have done something myself. Maybe I knew in my subconscious he was ill, and maybe I couldn't accept that. I was blind."

"But your subconscious did know, didn't it? That day we were in the sea together and I frightened you was the tip-off. And I damn well should have seen it."

She closed her eyes, smiling tiredly. "We both should have seen it. But when we were together, we only saw each other."

"That's true. Oh, darling, I will protect from this day on."

"And I'll protect you, Adolphus Prentice Wakefield."

"He needs to be confined, Bedelia. Then maybe he can be helped."

She nodded. "I wish my mother and father had told me how sick he was, that they were going to have him committed. I never knew that. But they tried very hard to be good parents. I've come to realize that over the years. My stepmother was kind to me, as was my father. It must have been a terrible burden to have the worry of Orton."

Dolph held her close.

The visit to the hospital was short. Dolph had been barely grazed. Bedelia's scratch was superficial.

By the time they reached his house, it was well past the time that they should have been at the chapel.

"I'll call and tell everyone we're on the way," Dolph said. "You get dressed." He paused when she hesitated on the stairs and looked at him, stricken. "What is it, love?"

"My dress. It's over at my place."

He smiled and shook his head. "It should be here. Bear told me that Kip went to your house to pick up the dress and bring it here." When she sagged in relief, her dismay turning to happiness, the breath caught in his throat. "Has anyone ever told you you're beautiful?"

"You have." She looked down, unaccustomedly shy.

"How wise of me." He wanted her desperately at that moment, but he would have been satisfied to hold her hand.

"I'd better hurry." Bedelia didn't move.

"Was there something else?" he asked huskily.

"Yes. I wondered if you'd kiss me."

"Of course." He sprinted across the hall and up the few stairs to stand on the step below her. "Umm, now we're eye-to-eye and mouth-to-mouth."

She pressed her lips to his. Then she pushed back from him, laughing and out of breath. "And we're late."

He laughed too, happy and free, watching her hurry up the stairs. "I'll call and see if they've been able to hold things together."

"You said that before, Wakefield. I think you're getting forgetful," she said impishly, and ran up to the bedroom.

Dolph heard the bedroom door close, but he didn't move. All at once he felt weak, drained. Bedelia was in his house, and she was safe. He moved slowly back down the stairs, his lips moving in prayer.

Bedelia stared into the mirror. Who is this stranger? she wondered. Her eyes seemed to be all pupil, her skin had a putty hue. Despite the shocked look, she was content. Dolph was downstairs. Soon they'd be married. But Orton . . . Why hadn't she realized how ill he was?

All at once she felt an insurmountable fatigue and sank onto the dressing-table stool.

Had her whole life been a facade? She should have seen what Orton was. Why hadn't her parents confided in her? Why hadn't she known at once that when she disappeared, she would hurt Dolph more than cutting him with a knife? Accepting that she'd run rather than face her problems gave her a harsh satisfaction. At least she was admitting the truth to herself.

For years she'd been building an empire, arranging her life with what she thought was good purpose. Yet not once in that time had she been perceptive enough to understand that her stepbrother was ill and in need of treatment. Instead of allowing Orton's distortions into her world, she should have taken steps to get him help. At that moment she saw many of her actions as counterproductive. Certainly all of her successes would have been dust if Dolph had rejected her. Her world would have crumbled around her.

Going into the bathroom, she showered and shampooed, moving quickly as thoughts tumbled through her mind.

Finally dressed in her champagne gown, she studied her reflection, not really seeing the froth of silk and lace, but only her eyes as she made a covenant with herself.

No more would she duck issues that were so deeply personal. Never again would she slough off uneasy sensations as she'd done with Orton. She'd take the time to examine every aspect, weigh the pros and cons.

And she would love Dolph with a whole love, a giving passion that would bring him joy. He was her life, and she would make him happy.

Orton would have the care he needed, the counseling, the security. She had the money for that.

Leaving the room, she moved toward the stairs just as Dolph came out of the other bedroom.

"I think I'm escorting the bride to her wedding," he said softly. Despite the lingering shadows in her eyes, he thought she was the most beautiful woman he'd ever seen. Her beauty was a font of love that came right from her toes and flooded her with its power.

At times like this his own failings as a lover and friend assailed him. Why hadn't he seen the rationale behind her departure from Nice? Had he been too involved in his own hurt to scrutinize the little clues all around him? The troubling thoughts had him shifting uncomfortably in his silk morning suit.

"What is it?" Bedelia asked, sensing he was bothered. "Is it about Orton?"

"No, love. I'm just mad at myself for not marrying you years ago."

She chuckled. "Poor baby."

"Well, I'm damned mad about it." All those years he'd really done little more than pay lip service to searching for her. He could have done more. He should have had Shim Locke on it all these years, instead of other investigators whose expertise he had no knowledge of. Pride had ridden him like a wild mustang, and he'd thought only of how he felt. If something had happened to Bedelia in that time, he would have blamed himself and rightly so. She had been young, impulsive. He'd been a man who'd reacted like a boy.

Bedelia saw the conflicting emotions race across his handsome face. He wasn't trying to hide anything from her. "You can't take all the blame for what's happened to us, you know."

"Maybe not. But I'm still kicking myself for the things I didn't do."

Bitter amusement laced his voice. Bedelia knew that Dolph was looking inward and that he hated the picture. She could empathize with that. "I know the feeling." She moved closer to him. "I should have known about Orton, but more importantly I should have known about you. I knew that you were sensitive and caring. You were that way with me. So how could I walk away from you and think I was doing both of us a favor? I was a fool." She tried to smile, but she couldn't bring it off.

He took her hand. "I've been doing a little soul-searching myself. It stings."

She nodded sympathetically, then gazed at him. "Have I told you you look very handsome?" Surprise held her immobile when she saw a flush color his cheeks. "Have I embarrassed you?"

"No. You pleased the hell out of me. I'm just not used to feeling this way, lady. In my world compliments are often as automatic as breathing. You take them with a box of salt, not a grain. But when they come from you, it knocks me over." He stroked her cheek. "You have a mysticism that controls my body. Just by a nuance you can drop or raise my blood pressure."

"Mighty, aren't I?"

"Oh, yes, you are." He lifted her hand and kissed the palm. "I promise you that Orton will get every care, the best therapists, and he will not be forgotten or shunted away."

Tears slipped down her cheeks. "Oh, Dolph, thank you. It would mean so much to my step-mother and father." She clutched his hand. "Why didn't I see it? And if I did, why did I hide it, even from myself?"

Her pain was his, and he ached for her. "We often do that to ourselves. I hid the anger and agony I felt when I lost you. I didn't communicate

it to anyone. I can see now how stupid that was."
He inhaled deeply. "And even when I was looking
for you, I didn't enlist the help of anyone who
really knew me, anyone I'd ever open up to and
perhaps give an important clue to finding you."
He sighed. "It was blind pride. It's damnable
stuff. It kept us apart for too long."

Her tears were a waterfall that she had to stem
with her hankie and Dolph's. "We're late, and now
I'll have to repair my face. We'll never get married."

"Yes, we will." He ushered her back into the
bedroom and hovered over her until she finished
redoing her makeup. He couldn't ignore the slight
shaking of her hand. But he squeezed it and
smiled at her. "I'm on edge too. It's been quite a
day. But we'll make it, together. Come on, lady.
I'm eager."

Her laugh was tremulous but genuine. "So am
I." She rose from the dressing table, pressed
trembling hands down the front of her gown, and
nodded. "Let's do it."

Dolph laughed and took her arm, then glanced
down when she paused. "Forget something?"

"Will I have to compete with all the beautiful
women you know in your business?"

"You've never had competition, Bedelia Fronsby.
And I think you know that. I love you, only you."
He swallowed hard at the radiance of her smile.
"And you're beautiful."

When they went down the stairs and outside,
Dolph looked around for a cab and found one in
front of the house.

The burly cab driver who'd helped him on the
waterfront got out of his cab and looked at them

over the top of it. "I figured you paid me for a few days anyway."

Dolph grinned. "Thanks for waiting. You're invited to the wedding."

"Yes, indeed you are," Bedelia said, preceding Dolph into the taxi. "Is this another person who will become your devoted friend, as Shim Locke has?"

Dolph smiled, glancing at the driver's identity shield. "I like Tomás Vilas. He's a man of courage and determination."

"Trust you to admire the attributes that you have in abundance," she said.

He caressed her hair. "Do you believe that about me?"

"I do."

"That's wonderful. Because I want to be all the virtues to you, my love, and that feeling's a first for me."

When they reached the chapel, they were both too bemused to realize it.

Only when Tomás opened the door did they step out.

A pacing Piers met them at the back of the church. "Lord, you're here. I was sure the priest would leave." He looked from one to the other. "I called The Pillory. They said putting back your time was no problem." When the door behind them opened and the cab driver appeared, Piers grinned at him.

Tomás Vilas nodded, his cap clutched between his hands. He slipped into a back pew in the old church.

"Take care of her, Piers," Dolph said.

"You bet."

Dolph kissed Bedelia once, twice.

"Hey, man, get out of here." Piers pushed his friend toward the chapel's nave.

In moments, they were ready. Bedelia took Piers's arm and walked down the aisle to meet her love.

Many of the words of the traditional service were lost on her as she gazed at the man at her side. All her dreams were coming true in that moment, all the happy times she'd envisioned for herself with Dolph telescoped down to that second. And if she felt a pang for past mistakes, it was more than soothed by the vows they exchanged. They had another grab for the brass ring, another chance for love, for discovering each other.

"You may kiss the bride."

Dolph looked at his wife and smiled. The world was Bedelia, and all else was icing. There would be pain and fire, but they would be surrounded by love. However long they lived, they would be together, and that was enough.

He lowered his head and kissed her.

In a flurry of good wishes they were on the street again, back in the cab.

The maitre d' was overly civil when they arrived at The Pillory.

"He's angry," Bedelia whispered wincing. "Not that I blame him. We're several hours past the scheduled time."

Dolph shrugged. "Damiene called and explained.

They could've said then that they couldn't accommodate us."

"Has anyone ever said that to you?"

His grin faded to a satirical twist. "A time or two, but only with you did it matter." He tightened his hold on her.

"Can we forget the hurts, Dolph? They seem to crop up time after time."

The maitre d' coughed delicately. "If you would follow me, please."

Dolph leaned down and kissed her cheek. "We're not in so much of a hurry that I don't have time to tell you that we will always settle any problem that comes up, together." He smiled, watching her closely. "We'll have time to talk later, Bedelia."

"Good. I want that," she said softly, then smiled when one of the guests approached her with good wishes.

"Here are the bride and groom. Let the orgy begin," Bear said, whisking Bedelia away from Dolph.

"Don't glare at him," Piers said, standing close to his friend. "I told him to do that. I wanted to speak to you. No sign of her stepbrother so far, but he could've landed anywhere. It's a long coastline. We're sure he got off the water, though, because the weather turned sour. The hurricane made landfall at South Carolina."

Dolph nodded. "Let Shim Locke and his people handle it. He'll find Orton." He didn't want any more shadows in Bedelia's eyes. She looked like a goddess in her champagne silk. His heart pounded out of rhythm when he thought about their future.

Piers studied his friend, then smiled. "I understand the need to be with your lady, my friend."

Dolph glanced at him and nodded. "I know you do. I remember how it was with you and Damiene." He pushed past some others and went to her side, leaning down to whisper in her ear. "We're going to a party, Mrs. Wakefield. And we're together."

Bedelia looked up, her smile widening. "And that's enough."

"Yes." He took her hand, threading his fingers through hers.

Since Piers, Damiene, Bear, Kip, their children, and Bear's family were the only guests, there was no receiving line. Dolph and Bedelia visited with their friends, had canapes and drinks with them, and stayed very close to each other.

When the food was served, a quartet took its place at the end of the room and played music of all eras, including ballads, waltzes, soft rock, and even concert music, done in modern style.

Before the cake was brought out, Dolph took Bedelia's hand and led her onto the dance floor. Other couples followed suit.

After a few minutes Bedelia broke free of Dolph and walked over to the leader of the quartet. "Would you play a polka? My husband and I would like to dance to it."

The leader smiled and turned to his group, whispering.

In moments the lively quickstep resounded through the room, making the guests smile, capturing their fancy.

Dolph watched his wife as she returned to him, grinning. He loved the light in her eyes, the impish smile. For a flash she was the nineteen-year-old Bedelia caught in a prism of time. "Think I can't do it?" he asked.

"Bet you can't."

"Oh? Fine. I'll bet you one long night in bed with no interruptions and no sleep that I can handle this."

"Why do you name the wager? It should be up to me."

He shook his head. "I dance. *You* pay the piper."

"Done." She put up her arms, and he caught her around the waist.

At first they were awkward, but the pull of the rhythm made their steps mesh, and they whirled around the floor, joining other laughing participants. The room rang with breathless laughter and music.

With a crash of cymbals the music ended, and Bedelia leaned against her husband, helpless with laughter, panting. "I—I needed that. It knocked off some of the rough edges, blew away the black clouds."

Dolph leaned down and kissed her, his breathing slowing. "You'll always have tortured memories of this day, but we'll remember joy too, sweetheart."

"Thanks to you." She closed her eyes for a second, then stared up at him. "I want to be alone with you."

"No sooner said than done." He gestured to Bear, who ambled over to them. "We're leaving."

Bear shook his head. "Can't. Have to cut the cake first." He grinned at Dolph's scowl. "I'll hurry it along."

"Do that."

They cut the cake, then the baker took over and sliced the rest.

Dolph looked at Bear and Piers. "Now we're leaving."

"I don't blame you," Piers said, then groaned as Patrick Adolphus put his hand in the cake.

Bedelia and Dolph laughed.

"Get going. We'll handle this—" Bear grimaced and lifted his son's hand from the cake, "I think."

"Good. Let's get out of here, love." Dolph grinned when his wife laughed. "So long, boys. Have fun with the cake."

"Thanks." Piers and Bear spoke at the same time, maneuvering the twins away from the confection.

Dolph and Bedelia made quick good-byes to the others and left.

That night they made love, caressing and murmuring love words to each other over and over, overjoyed at their oneness, relieved that their life could begin anew and that only death could part them.

"I love you."

Neither knew who said it.

Nine months later Dolph and Bedelia entertained their good friends, the Kenmores and the Larrabys.

"No one has babies nine months after their

marriage any more," Bedelia said, frowning at her distended belly. "That was pretty common with our mothers and grandmothers, but not today!"

She looked morosely at her guests, and two great tears slipped down her cheeks. Bear and Piers leaped to their feet and rushed to kneel next to her chair. They patted her hands and scowled at their wives who were laughing.

"Dolph, get in here," Piers said bitingly. "And, Damiene, stop it. I hate to see her cry."

Damiene laughed harder.

"Lorette! Bring cold cloths," Bear said, his voice rising. "Kip, cut it out. She might make herself sick."

Kip grinned and shook her head.

"Is she crying?" Dolph called from the butler's pantry.

"Yes," Kip said, laughing even harder when Bear took the edge of the Irish linen tablecloth and wiped Bedelia's eyes.

Damiene dried her own eyes with her hankie. "I loved it when she did this in the taxi the other day. The driver had ten fits."

"She does this all the time," Dolph said, returning to the dining room. "You should be used to it by now. The least little thing sets her off. She's cried buckets since she became pregnant."

Bedelia nodded as Dolph dried her face. "I—I hate it." She smiled as she gulped the words.

"Damn. I still don't like it." Bear looked wary but relieved when he sank back into his chair.

Piers sat down and kissed his wife. "But your unholy glee was uncalled-for."

Dolph smiled at the other two women, ignoring

Bedelia for a moment when she pulled on his sleeve. "Oh. Sorry. What is it, darling?"

"Time to go to the hospital," she said. She laughed through her tears when Dolph paled and sank to his knees. "Gotcha," she whispered, patting his head.

After the birth Dolph bent over Bedelia, his face still pale. "She's beautiful, my love."

"Make sure the nurses watch her the way they should. I saw them all looking at you instead." Bedelia yawned hugely. "I feel good . . . thin . . . and tired." She touched his cheek with one finger. "I love you, father of my daughter." Her eyes closed and she slept, a smile on her face.

"I love you for all time, Bedelia Wakefield," Dolph said quietly. "You melted my heart and gave me warmth forever."

He kissed his wife and never even noticed the sighing nurses clustered at the door, straining for glimpses of the famous actor.

THE EDITOR'S CORNER

In publishing a series such as LOVESWEPT we couldn't function without timetables, schedules, deadlines. It seems we're always working toward one, only to reach it then strive for another. I mention the topic because many of you write and ask us questions about the way we work and about how and when certain books are published. Just consider this Editor's Corner as an example. I'm writing this in early April, previewing our October books, which will run in our September books, which will be on sale in August. The books you're reading about were scheduled for publication at least nine months earlier and were probably written more than a year before they reach your hands! Six books a month means seventy-two a year, and we're into our seventh year of publication. That's a lot of books and a lot of information to try to keep up with. Amazingly, we do keep up—and so do our authors. We enjoy providing you with the answer to a question about a particular book or author or character. Your letters mean a lot to us.

In our ongoing effort to extend the person-to-person philosophy of LOVESWEPT, we are setting up a 900 number through which you can learn what's new—and what's old—with your favorite authors! Next month's Editor's Corner will have the full details for you.

Kay Hooper's most successful series for us to date has been her *Once Upon a Time . . .* novels. These modern-day fairy tales have struck a chord with you, the readers, and your enjoyment of the books has delighted and inspired Kay. Her next in this series is LOVESWEPT #426, **THE LADY AND THE LION,** and it's one of Kay's sizzlers. Keith Donovan and Erin Prentice first speak to each other from their adjacent hotel balconies, sharing secrets and desperate murmurings in the dark. Kay creates a moody, evocative, emotionally charged atmosphere in which these two kindred spirits fall in love before they ever meet. But when they finally do set eyes on each other, they know without having to speak that they've found their destinies. This wonderful story will bring out the true romantic in all of you!

We take you from fairy tales to fairyland this month! Our next LOVESWEPT, #427, **SATIN SHEETS AND STRAWBERRIES** by Marcia Evanick, features a golden-haired nymph of a heroine named Kelli SantaFe. Hero Logan Sinclair does a double take when he arrives at what looks like Snow White's cottage in search of his aunt and uncle—and finds a bewitching woman dressed as a fairy. Kelli runs her business from her home and at first resents Logan's interference and the tug-of-war he wages for his relatives, whom she'd taken in and treated like the family

(continued)

she'd always wanted. Logan is infuriated by her stubbornness, yet intrigued by the woman who makes him feel as though his feet barely touch the ground. Kelli falls hard for Logan, who can laugh at himself and rescue damsels in distress, but who has the power to shatter her happiness. You'll find you're enchanted by the time Kelli and Logan discover how to weave their dreams together!

All of us feel proud and excited whenever we publish a new author in the line. The lady whose work we're introducing you to next month is a talented, hardworking mother of five who strongly believes in the importance of sprinkling each day with a little romance. We think Olivia Rupprecht does just that with **BAD BOY OF NEW ORLEANS,** LOVESWEPT #428. I don't know about you, but some of my all-time favorite romances involve characters who reunite after years apart. I find these stories often epitomize the meaning of true love. Well, in **BAD BOY OF NEW ORLEANS** Olivia reunites two people whose maddening hunger for each other has only deepened with time. Hero Chance Renault can still make Micah Sinclair tremble, can still make her burn for his touch and cry out for the man who had loved her first. But over time they've both changed, and a lot stands between them. Micah feels she must prove she can survive on her own, while Chance insists she belongs to him body and soul. Their journey toward happiness together is one you won't want to miss!

Joan Elliott Pickart never ceases to amaze me with the way she is able to provide us with winning romance after winning romance. She's truly a phenomenon, and we're pleased and honored to bring you her next LOVESWEPT, #429, **STORM-ING THE CASTLE.** While reunited lovers have their own sets of problems to overcome, when two very different people find themselves falling in love, their long-held beliefs, values, and lifestyles become an issue. In **STORMING THE CASTLE,** Dr. Maggie O'Leary finds her new hunk of a neighbor, James-Steven Payton, to be a free spirit, elusive as the wind and just as irresistible. Leave it to him to choose the unconventional over the customary way of doing things. But Maggie grew up with a father who was much the same, whose devil-may-care ways often brought heartache. James-Steven longs to see the carefree side of Maggie, and he sets out to get her to smell the flowers and to build sand castles without worrying that the tide will wash them away. Though Maggie longs to join her heart to his, she knows they must first find a common ground. Joan handles this tender story beautifully. It's a real heart-warmer!

One author who always delivers a fresh, innovative story is Mary Kay McComas. Each of her LOVESWEPTs is unique and imaginative—never the same old thing! In **FAVORS,** LOVESWEPT #430, Mary Kay has once again let her creative juices flow, and

(continued)

the result is a story unlike any other. Drawing on her strength in developing characters you come to know intimately and completely, Mary Kay serves up a romance filled with emotion and chock full of fun. Her tongue-in-cheek portrayal of several secondary characters will have you giggling, and her surprise ending will add the finishing touch to your enjoyment of the story. When agent Ian Walker is asked to protect a witness as a favor to his boss, he considers the job no more appealing than baby-sitting—until he meets Trudy Babbitt, alias Pollyanna. The woman infuriates him by refusing to believe she's in danger—and ignites feelings in him he'd thought were long dead. Trudy sees beneath Ian's crusty exterior and knows she can transform him with her love. But first they have to deal with the reality of their situation. I don't want to give away too much, so I'll just suggest you keep in mind while reading **FAVORS** that nothing is exactly as it seems. Crafty Mary Kay pulls a few aces from her sleeve!

One of your favorite authors—and ours—Billie Green returns to our lineup next month with **SWEET AND WILDE**, #431. Billie has always been able to capture that indefinable quality that makes a LOVESWEPT romance special. In her latest for us, she throws together an unlikely pair of lovers, privileged Alyson Wilde and streetwise Sid Sweet and sends them on an incredible adventure. You might wonder what a blue-blooded lady could have in common with a bail bondsman and pawnshop owner, but Billie manages to keep her characters more than a little bit interested in each other. When thirteen-year-old Lenny, who is Alyson's ward, insists that his friend Sid Sweet is a great guy and role model, Alyson decides she has to meet the tough-talking man for herself. And cynical Sid worries that Good Samaritan Alyson has taken Lenny on only as her latest "project." With Lenny's best interests at heart, they go with him in search of his past and end up discovering their own remarkable future—one filled with a real love that is better than any of their fantasies.

Be sure to pick up all six books next month. They're all keepers!
Sincerely,

Susann Brailey

Susann Brailey
Editor
LOVESWEPT
Bantam Books
666 Fifth Avenue
New York, NY 10103

FAN OF THE MONTH

Sandra Beattie

How did I come to be such a fan of LOVESWEPT romances? It was by accident, really. My husband was in the Australian Navy and we were moving once again to another state. I wanted some books to read while we stayed in the motel, so I went to a second-hand bookstore in search of some Silhouette romances. I spotted some books I hadn't seen before, and after reading the back covers I decided to buy two. I asked the saleslady to set the rest aside in case I wanted them later. I read both books that night and was hooked. I raced back to the store the next day and bought the rest. I've been a fan of LOVESWEPT ever since.

My favorite authors are Sandra Brown, Kay Hooper, Iris Johansen, Fayrene Preston, Joan Elliott Pickart, and Mary Kay McComas. The thing I like about LOVESWEPT heroes is that they are not always rich and handsome men, but some are struggling like us. I cry and laugh with the people in the books. Sometimes I become them and feel everything that they feel. The love scenes are just so romantic that they take my breath away. But then some of them are funny as well.

I'm thirty-four years old, the mother of three children. I love rock and roll, watching old movies, and snuggling up to my husband on cold, rainy nights. If there is one thing I can pass on to other readers, it is that you can't let everything get you down. When I feel depressed, I pick up a LOVESWEPT and curl up in a chair for a while and just forget about everything. Then when I get up again, the world doesn't look so bad anymore. Try it, it really works!